FILTHY HOUSEWIVES

EDITED BY VIOLET BLUE

D1744260

DIGITA PUBLICATIONS

DigitaPub.com

Published in the United States by Digita Publications, San Francisco, California, DigitaPub.com.

Published in the United States.
Cover design: Violet Blue
Text design: Violet Blue
Logo art: Violet Blue
First Edition.
ISBN: 9781520928722
10 9 8 7 6 5 4 3 2 1

TABLE OF CONTENTS

INTRODUCTION

Over a decade of editing erotic anthologies, publishing literally hundreds of writers, and more submissions than I dare recount—you might say that I'm a bit picky when it comes to erotica. Just a little.

Truthfully, I'm a lot picky. Which is why, after ending my ten-year run editing the prestigious (and award-snatching) series *Best Women's Erotica*, I wanted to do some very specific things with the erotica collections I'd envisioned and always wanted to make.

Don took me into Kurt's line, and then he put a packet of mints on the storm-gray conveyor belt. That was all we had. The woman in front of us paid for her groceries—what a lot of cat food she had—and Don smiled at Kurt as the youth rang up our solitary item.

"Can you take a break?" Don asked.

There was nobody behind us. The other checkers seemed to have the traffic flow under control.

"Sure, Sir. Did you…" he looked at the small container of mints. "Did you need help with your groceries?" He asked this with a straight face.

Don laughed. "No, of course not. I need to teach my wife a lesson, and I'd like your help." Kurt's gaze flickered over me. I'd had a day already, and it was only eleven in the morning. I wondered what I looked like. Could he tell I'd already been paddled in front of my boss? Could he guess that my ass was throbbing under my clothes? Could he smell that I was so turned on I could have lit someone's cigarette just by blowing on it?

Kurt turned off the number on his check stand and went over to the manager's office at the rear of the store.

--Alison Tyler, "Out Of Luck"

Those things are all in *Filthy Housewives*. The list begins with my desire to handpick writers: the best of today's erotic authors, focused on areas in which they excel. Authors who are hungry for making a story compelling, imbued with the values savvy erotica readers demand to craft sex-positive, consent-conscious, intense sexual fantasies with characters that make sense, and worlds that wholly lack the sexist trappings of erotic smut that we usually turn to for wilder fantasies.

Next, I wanted to assemble highly literary smutfests on specific topics, ones that address a central turn-on. Like the deviant, crafty modern wife. What happens when we introduce her to the usual wife-themed fantasies? Well, she gets what she wants—and sometimes what she deserves, in the best of ways. And so do we.

"Marcus," I called down the stairs. "Can you help me out up here?"

"I thought you had Thad," my husband called back after a moment. I could hear the sound of jazz playing.

I motioned for Thad to come closer to me. I slid one hand into his pants and started to touch his cock. "I do have Thad," I yelled back. "I have his big hard cock in my hand."

There was a blast of happy notes as a horn player took a solo. I waited and then called down. "When he's done fucking me, he's going to fuck you."

The music abruptly went off.

I heard footsteps on the stairs. I hurried to push Thad down on the bed. Marcus moved faster than I expected. He was suddenly there, right by the bed, as I shifted aside my copper-colored panties and began to lower myself on Thad's glorious dick.

"What… what's going on?" Marcus asked.

I pushed my hips up and then slid down Thad's pole. "I'm fucking Thad," I said.

I've been calling what the women in those stories do "modern wifecraft" in my head all throughout working on this book, from the first sketches of these stories to the back and forth with the authors, all the way until today's finishing touches and final markups from the editors. You may think it's a nod to "witchcraft." Or perhaps it conjures visions of a secret agent wife, trading her daily wifecraft for a three-letter-agency's tradecraft for its best spies.

Both are correct. The fantasy that we might all possess their capacity for sexual voraciousness and courage to reach for the brass rings within our own secrets. And our dream of that partner in crime who rises to the challenge of meeting us there, in our sexual secrets.

It's a sublime fantasy, the suburban housewife endowed with extraordinary sexual adventures, and we get vicarious empowerment from these fantasies. It's a rush that'll make you want to cross and uncross your legs while reading, I assure you.

"Jesus," says Raymond softly. We have never done anything kinky together. In our four-year marriage, we've only ever fucked in the dark. This has always confused me. Here we live in paradise. He could have taken me outside, by the reflecting pond. He could have screwed me in our mirrored dining room or in the massive shower with the four big heads. Instead, he has treated me like one of his treasured *objets d'art*. With kid gloves. With reverence. But never the way I want.

"What do you think about the way she looks?"

Raymond doesn't seem to have an answer to that. At least, not right away. I hear the sound of his glass being set on the coffee table. I hear him walking around me.

"She looks..." he starts, "she looks..." he tries again, "she looks so fucking sexy." His voice is hoarse.

I sag with relief, that is, until Della continues: "Did you know she likes anal sex?"

Raymond seems to realize he's supposed to respond, because he clears his throat and says, "No. We've never done that."

--*Tasha Waters, "Home Sweet Home"*

The filthy housewife is a guilty pleasure fantasy, and an immortal vehicle for all kinds of porny flights of fancy. Thank goodness for that, because we need all the permission to dwell on the forbidden we can get these days.

The filthy housewives between these pages take us by the hand and grant us permission to go with them, further than we'd go in real life. All the way until we're red reading this book on the subway or plane, or we can't wait to send a chapter or read a snippet aloud to someone we'd like to fuck. And that's the point.

So when Max showed up like that before I'd even poured the white wine, I felt mortified. How could I be expected to watch what was going on in the neighborhood if I couldn't keep control of the comings-and-goings in my own house?

With all eyes on him, he checked his watch and stammered, "I didn't realize…"

"You didn't realize that you'd ignored what your wife told you?" Tammy sneered at him. I turned to look at her, surprised by her tone.

"You didn't realize that if you came to the meeting, you'd have to dress like a lady?" asked Betsey. My head swiveled in her direction. I felt as if I were watching a tennis match, one in which Max was the ball.

"You didn't realize that we were going to strip you down and use your cock for our own pleasure?"

Max's face showed his emotions clearly. He seemed as shocked as I was—but he also looked interested. What man wouldn't be? Four women were eying him as if he were the best bit of beefcake they'd ever seen.

"If you want to stay," said Tammy, "you'll have to pay the price."

--Jewel Rodriguez, "Neighborhood Wives Watch"

As many of my regular readers know, I used to review porn for a living. And I wrote all about it, in a book for women who watch porn and in many articles for major magazines about those women, and what people think it all means. Oprah had me come on her show and talk about it, and then hang out with her and her audience for a morning of Q and A about porn, and women, and what we think of porn.

One thing we all agreed on: porn generally sucks. *Fifty Shades* is a joke and an insult, but we all read it. And why not, it's like the porno-fanfic version of a bag of chips! We keep eating even though we know it'll make our stomachs hurt later. It's better than the porn version of a healthy snack—but why not just make some good litporn instead?

So that's what we set out to do, myself and the authors of *Filthy Housewives*. We made the porn we want to see.

Seriously? Shakespeare Tan. Someone got paid to create that name. Think about that for a moment.

The truth was that I didn't care. Sheila knew I didn't care. I'd gone beyond pretending to care.

I answered the call with an impatient sigh, I'll admit that. The (paint) chips were down, so to speak. I was fifty shades past the ability to comment. And I stayed that way. Because what I saw when the Skype window opened was Sheila tied to our antique four-poster bed. There were three men in the room, men I'd never seen before.

One was dark-haired and tall, with vibrantly colored tattoos spiraling all over his pale skin. Another had blond hair to his shoulders and was what I'd consider a surfer type, a real all-American stud. The last was slightly off-screen.

I could only see his big dick aimed right at my wife's face.

"Hi, Honey," Sheila said, and she flittered her fingers at me. She couldn't actually wave. Not tied down like that.

--Dante Davidson, "Eggshell, Ecru and Linen"

I think it's really interesting that both witchcraft shows and spycraft shows are growing in popularity, at a time when lots of us—in all genders and orientations—are reclaiming porn from the people who produce crap, and making it our own. The female characters on both witch and spy shows don't discover their powers until they're in their 20s—until they're grown women. These characters started as wallflowers, as skeptics, and yes, as housewives.

What they come to discover is that there is power in sharing their secrets.

From myself, and all the authors who worked to create the people and worlds in *Filthy Housewives*: We hope you feel as turned on and powerful sinking into the fantasies in this collection as strongly as the love, hotness and mirth we all poured into it.

Violet Blue
San Francisco

OUT OF LUCK

BY ALISON TYLER

Fucking Monday.

Some people's Monday morning blues involve bumper-to-bumper traffic. Others oversleep or run out of coffee or simply would rather be anywhere else but at work.

My Monday involved a spanking, a blowjob, and a whipping by a neighbor I'd had a crush on for years. But I'm getting ahead of myself.

"I don't know what happened," I said, dabbing my eyes as I stared at my sad face in the mirror. "I'm usually on top of things." I tried to force the corners of my lips to turn up. The smile melted in front of my eyes.

"Really." Don's voice wasn't simply chilled. His voice had spent the night in a deep freeze out in our garage.

"This just isn't my lucky day," I sniffled, continuing to try to make myself presentable. But cosmetics will only go so far. My mascara was running, and every time I wiped away tears, new crystal droplets spilled free. The week had started out in a normal enough fashion. Except that my Monday went far worse than I'd initially anticipated. I'd mistaken the deadline on my latest project. Instead of being due the following week, the proposal was supposed to be on my boss's desk in… oh, seven minutes. It was like a countdown to doom.

There wasn't even enough time to make up a proper excuse.

I'd called Don from the ladies' room, desperate. "What do I say to her?" I asked next, grasping for the gold ring of hope that my husband would come through for me. He's the kind of guy people look to for advice—no matter the subject.

"Put her on the phone," Don said.

"I'm in the powder room," I confessed. I could imagine the disappointed look on his face. He would have understood that I was hiding out. Not the most professional way to behave. What was he doing now? Spinning one of his gold cufflinks. Adjusting his charcoal silk tie.

"Go to your boss's office, call me from her phone, and explain that I'd like to speak to her."

I stared at my tear-streaked reflection in the mirror. How could I do what he was asking? My boss knew Don from those mandatory-fun types of work occasions: Softball in the park, the art department against the sales team. Picnic by the lake on the Fourth of July, everyone behaving properly until tipsiness took over. But this was something different. He'd never insinuated himself into my career before. Still, I held onto the wishful thinking that he'd save me.

After five years as his wife, I should have known better.

Somehow I managed to blot my tears, fix my face, and stumble into Chelsea's office. The tears remained right there under the surface, but I thought I had the situation at least partially under control. My boss didn't even look up when I entered. With her phone cradled delicately between her shoulder and her ear, she was taking notes in rapid fashion on a sleek chrome laptop. I stood before her desk, waiting for her to notice me, and feeling like a naughty schoolgirl destined for a principal's wrath.

I had a loathe/hate relationship with my boss. She was the kind of vixen I've despised since high school homecoming days. No princess for her. Chelsea was an ice queen all the way to the tips of her toenails. Although she always looked factory-sealed perfect, I'd never been able to figure out when she had the time to primp. She seemed permanently stapled to the corporate ladder.

Didn't she think she was so great, her cinnamon-hued hair short and sleek in the latest pixie cut, her expensive cashmere turtleneck clinging to her perfect physique? She was wearing diamond-and-sapphire earrings—obviously to set off the striking blue of her eyes. Why did she always look so put together? I shifted from one foot to the other, aware that I needed to straighten the seams on my stockings, aware that I'd cried off nearly all of my eye makeup.

Chelsea kept on talking while I observed her every move.

As a creative type, I couldn't have stepped into her shoes if I'd wanted to, which I didn't. But I *did* want to do my job well, and I'd flailed. Chelsea finally hung up the phone and looked at me with exasperation. In a halting voice, I explained the situation. Chelsea watched me dispassionately as I dialed my husband. Then she took the phone from my trembling hand and said, "Don, good morning," in a crisp, clear, I-sing-in-the-Sunday-choir voice.

I tried to imagine what Don was saying to her. Perhaps I ought to have guessed, but my brain was so far gone by this point. When Chelsea laughed, I broke from my worry and almost smiled. Don had come through! Don was making everything better!

I glanced at the framed photo of a French beach on one of

Chelsea's walls. The sun suddenly felt as if it were shining on me with the same shimmery brightness it did in that snapshot. Don—my magic man. Don—my king. What had he said? That we'd spent the weekend at our cabin without any access to devices? That I'd left the project in his car, and he'd driven it to work without thinking? That our dog ate my... Then Chelsea hit a button and I heard my husband's voice on the intercom, and all of my worst fears were realized.

"Have her naked standing in the corner by the time I get there," he said, "I'll heat her ass for her while you watch." I blanched and felt as if I might pass out. Chelsea disconnected the line and looked at me. She no longer appeared exasperated. Her eyes narrowed as she waited for me to obey my husband's command. I considered pretending the whole thing was joke, a horrible, hideous joke gone wrong. But to my dismay Chelsea was coming around to my side of the desk and undoing the row of buttons on my stupid Peter Pan collar shirt. Why had I bought this thing? What type of a coward wore shirts like this? I wanted armor. I wanted chain mail.

She said, "Don and I had a very interesting talk at the last picnic. He told me what a precocious sub you were, and I was intrigued to hear about the dirty games the two of you play."

"He said...? He told you?" *Why would he have done that?*

She paused to look directly into my eyes, and once more I was shocked by the pure cobalt blue. "Because you need someone to take a firm hand with you. That's what he told me then. He was looking out for you. And he must have sensed in me the ability..." she pulled my shirt off and then undid my pale, seashell-colored bra. She unzipped my navy skirt and yanked it down my thighs along with my stockings. I had no way to process the situation—

Yes, Don is in charge of me at home, and yes every so often I've been in situations where he has invited others to join us, but I hadn't thought one of the others would ever be my boss. If he'd even made the suggestion, I would have fought against the idea as hard as I possibly could. This is probably why he arranged for the situation to unfold out of my control.

My husband works only a few buildings away from mine. By the time he showed up, I was naked and Chelsea was enjoying herself tormenting me. In one hand she held a clip, the kind used to pinch together reports, and she was discussing how it might feel if she were to place that cruel-looking clamp on my clit.

"What do you think we should do to you?" she asked as Don entered the room. I could feel his force as he looked at me. "Something serious so you can really remember your deadlines in the future. Don't you think?"

Don locked the door behind him and then came to my side. There he was in his deep gray suit, somber expression except for a knowing spark in his eyes. "You know this is for your own good," he said, "Don't you?" I nodded, helpless, as he led me to Chelsea's bright yellow sofa and sat down. I stood in front of him until he spread me over his lap. I was going to get a spanking in front of my boss. I was going to get a spanking from my husband in the middle of Monday morning at work in the front of my stick-up-her-ass boss. I was going to...

Don rubbed his palm over my asscheeks, and I felt myself grow immediately wet. He was touching me almost casually, as if he were petting a fat lazy housecat instead of preparing me for a spanking.

Preparing me. That's a laugh. He was about to give me a spanking! My mind took off again. Oh, god. How do I get myself into situations like this? Why do I get myself into...?

Don's hand connected with my ass as he delivered the first brutal spank, and I cried out. Chelsea was on me immediately. "You are at work, young lady," she said. "Make another noise like that, and we'll have a problem."

Don was making plenty of noise by smacking his palm against my ass, but I didn't issue a squeak after that. I kept as still as I possibly could, and I did my best to show both my husband and my boss that I really could behave when I put my mind to it. I tried to think of what I might say after the spanking was over, how I might somehow redeem myself, but there really was no way. My husband was giving me a bare-bottomed spanking in front of my boss, and she was always going to remember this. Whenever she saw me in the hall, she would smirk and recall the way my ass had grown neon red under my husband's stern blows.

As someone accustomed to being on the receiving end of this sort of punishment, I felt I did a fairly adept job at not flailing about. But Don really pushed me to my limits. When he stopped spanking me, I felt myself sigh in relief. It was over. He was going to take pity on me. He was going to stop the punishment.

Unfortunately, Don was simply adjusting me so that my thighs were slightly parted. Then I felt his fingers start to pat my pussy, hard enough to make me gasp, but soft enough to ... oh, holy fuck... to get me off. He pat me with his four fingers held stiffly together, and he employed a rhythm that seemed to match the beating of my heart. Chelsea moved closer to me. I could smell her classy perfume—what was it? *Shalimar? White Shoulders?* She moved behind me and I guessed that she was getting a long, good look at my private parts.

"You try," Don said.

"Oh, I don't know," Chelsea responded in mock politeness, as if turning down a second slice of pie.

"I insist," Don said gentlemanly, and then I felt my boss spanking my pussy.

There was nothing I could do then, no way I could hide. Her fingers spanked me expertly between my legs, and I came without even realizing I was going to. I came like a wind through an orchard, rustling every leaf. I had to bite into my arm to stifle a moan. Chelsea laughed at me, and I felt tears spark the corners of my eyes once more. She laughed at what a little pain-sub-slut I was, and I felt more embarrassed than I'd ever been in my life.

Climaxing for Chelsea was far worse than being spanked in front of her. Because now she really knew me. She knew what control Don had over me. She knew I loved every fucking second of his tormenting mind games.

She. Knew.

Don stood me up in front of him, and then he walked me to the corner. *Fuck.* He was going to make me do corner time in Chelsea's office? Had my depths of wallowing not reached deep enough? Apparently not. Right before I faced the corner, I peeked over my shoulder and saw him sitting back on the sofa. All the while I stood on display and felt ridiculously sorry for myself, Don engaged in a friendly conversation with Chelsea. It was as if they'd met at a coffee shop. Bumped into one another when they'd least expected to.

"We'd love for you to come over some time," I heard him saying. "We could take turns with her. I'd love to fuck her while she eats you out. Would you be into something like that?"

Chelsea assured him that she would, and I had the instant vision of burying my face between her creamy thighs and licking her split. Maybe I'd enjoy tongue-fucking the ice queen. Chelsea definitely warmed up to the idea.

"In fact," Don continued, "you might even like to stop by tonight for this little party…"

Tonight? What was tonight? Oh, god, yes. Tonight was our neighborhood Earth Day Potluck. I had been selected to host this year's event at our house. Was Chelsea really going to come over for that? While my mind was lost in these queries, Chelsea came over to me with my clothes in her hands.

"Take the rest of the day off," she said. "We'll reschedule the project until next Monday. That should give you plenty of time to catch up—and to be able to sit down again." There was that knowing smile. I dressed and tried my best to act however it is you're supposed to act in situations like this. I don't know if I succeeded or failed. My bottom was burning. My face was hot. My pussy was wet. What more did these two doms want from me?

Don politely said his goodbyes to Chelsea, and then he led me out of the office and to the elevator. I felt as if I had been put through a tornado. My whole world was distorted. Even the walls of the elevator looked wavery.

"What are we…?" I stammered. "Where are we?" When why how? What did I really want to know? I wanted to know Don's plans.

I wanted to know what he was going to do to me next. I shouldn't have been so eager to find out.

In the elevator, Don handed me the grocery bill.

I shut my eyes. I had meant to pay the bill. I always paid the bill on time. At least, I always *usually* paid the bill on time. But the last time I'd been late (one of those always usually times) Don had told me what would happen if I fucked up again.

"Haven't I gone through enough?" I asked.

When will I learn? Why can't I keep my fool mouth shut?

"That's an interesting question," Don said. "I'll have to think about that while you're blowing Kurt."

Holy fucking fuck.

Kurt was the adorable checker with the dark blue eyes who worked at the grocery store. The one who always smiled at me. The one who clearly thought I was cute with a capital Q. And I was about to let him see who I really was. A submissive who would do anything her dominant man said. The only thing that calmed me down was the fact that Don was in charge. I would do what he required, and I didn't have to orchestrate anything on my own.

That doesn't mean I didn't cry on the way to the grocery store. I threw my own pity party, staring forlornly out the window, as Don said, "I told you. I told you the next time you were late paying the bill I would march you in there myself and make you blow that surfer boy you bat your lashes at."

He had said that. Sometimes when he cuffed me to the bed at night, when he spanked me with his belt or disciplined me with his paddle, he'd spell out scenarios exactly like that one. To my chagrin, I would always come. He knew me so well. He knew precisely how to take me over the edge with his words and his actions. But up until now, I'd never believed he'd go through with this particular threat.

Is that really true? If I hadn't at least partially believed him, would I have put him to the test like this? Not paying. Not doing my work. Not…

We were at the store. Don dragged me from the car and through the pneumatic doors. I felt that cold rush of supermarket air hit me, which was a welcome sensation because I was burning up with mortification. The back of my neck felt hot and wet. My cheekbones were on fire. I drew in a big, deep breath of air and then realized where Don was dragging me. To checkstand seven. To Kurt.

Oh, fuck, oh, fuck, oh, fuck.

Kurt couldn't have been a nicer guy. He had worked at the store all through college and was now saving money for a surfing trip to Australia—"before real life starts," he always said with a laugh. Like he knew a thing or two about real life. Like he was in no rush to join the realm of the grown-up world. He never failed to compliment me, always helped me with my bags to the car. Don took me into Kurt's line, and then he put a packet of mints on the storm-gray conveyor belt. That was all we had. The woman in front of us paid for her groceries—what a lot of cat food she had—and Don smiled at Kurt as the youth rang up our solitary item.

"Can you take a break?" Don asked.

There was nobody behind us. The other checkers seemed to have the traffic flow under control.

"Sure, Sir. Did you…" he looked at the small container of mints. "Did you need help with your groceries?" He asked this with a straight face.

Don laughed. "No, of course not. I need to teach my wife a lesson, and I'd like your help." Kurt's gaze flickered over me. I'd had a day already, and it was only eleven in the morning. I wondered what I looked like. Could he tell I'd already been paddled in front of my boss? Could he guess that my ass was throbbing under my clothes? Could he smell that I was so turned on I could have lit someone's cigarette just by blowing on it?

Kurt turned off the number on his check stand and went over to the manager's office at the rear of the store. While Don and I stood there waiting, my husband flipped opened the top of the tin and slid one of the small, round mints onto my tongue. "Suck," he said. I closed my eyes and sucked. When Kurt returned, the three of us went out of the store. Don led us around to the back of the grocery—to the dumpsters and piles of dismantled cardboard boxes. There was a half a container of wilted celery, a slew of cabbage leaves littering the ground like deflated balloons on the morning after a party.

"You're not married," Don said matter-of-factly to Kurt.

"No Sir."

"Well, one day you might very well be. And there's a chance you'll find yourself with a disobedient wife who needs a tune up every now and again."

Kurt's eyes found mine once more. I was a wreck, trembling all over. This was really happening. I was actually going to do this.

"I hope you'll remember this day," Don said, and he pushed me to my knees on the gritty asphalt and motioned for Kurt to undo his trousers.

"Sir?" Kurt seemed to be in shock.

"My wife needs to be taught a lesson," Don repeated. "So I'm going to have her blow you. I hope you don't mind."

Kurt's mouth opened. He seemed to want to say something, but no words came out.

"She'll drain you dry. She's a good cocksucker—I've taught her well. And then I'll take her home and paddle her for enjoying the taste of another man's come. I hope you don't mind helping us out."

Kurt looked from Don to me to Don again.

"And she's…?" he started.

"Oh, yes. She's okay with this. She would never have been late with the grocery bill if she didn't want your dick in her mouth. She knew the price of being a sloppy little slut. Now she's paying. Next time, I'll let you spank her if you'd like."

Kurt's hand moved tentatively to his fly. "That's right," said Don encouragingly. "Go on."

The surfer boy undid the button and the zipper and pulled out his dick. He was hard already. Don pushed me forward. I stumbled on my knees, feeling the rough pebbles in the asphalt biting into my skin. Then I opened my mouth and started to suck Kurt. He sighed at my mint-cooled breath. He didn't seem to know what to do with his hands, so Don said, "You call the shots, kid. You fuck her face as hard or slow as you like. She'll stay with you. She can handle this type of situation like a pro. Throat fuck her if you'd like, or take things easy. She's trained to please."

I blushed further at that, thinking of different ways Don has punished me in the past. Like the time we ran out of liquor during one of his poker parties, and he passed me around the table, letting each of his buddies have a hand spanking my ass. He sent me out for gin wearing only my raincoat over my naked body with the knowledge that when I returned, the man who'd won the last round was going to fuck me up the ass.

Blowing a boy in the alley behind the grocery store was like icing compared to some of Don's tricks.

Kurt started to moan, and I worked my tongue along the underside of his cock.

I sucked him sweetly, because I liked him. I wanted this to feel good. I used my tongue to trace designs on his cock, and then I really worked the tip, creating an oral vacuum for the blond pretty boy. He came quickly. My guess was nothing like this had ever happened to him before.

"Swallow," Don instructed, and I drained him dry and licked my lips. Then I waited, and Don stood me up and shook Kurt's hand. The surfer looked like he wanted to say something to me—maybe thank you, maybe something else—but Don just patted him on the shoulder and led me around the store to the parking lot in front. I was in a daze. What was Don going to do next? He handed me over another mint, and he said, "There's a bag in the back seat. Open it up."

He was already driving us home. I reached around and picked up the small paper bag. The contents rattled as I set the bag on my lap. Was it a present for me? What could be inside? I unfolded the paper lip and peered within.

Jesus.

Inside the bag were shards of a mug. I knew the mug. It said, "World's Best Dad." Or it had said that once upon a time. I'd accidentally broken the hideous thing when I'd been to our neighbor's house the week before for a quick cup of coffee. How had the pottery pieces managed to find their way in that small bag to Don?

"Andy told me what happened," Don said as I shut the bag once more and set it miserably at my feet. "He said you were doing too many things at once. Checking your phone, drinking the coffee, trying to find your keys. You know how I feel about multitasking."

I sat there in stunned silence. What a fucking day this was turning out to be.

"So tonight, during the potluck, you're going to make it up to Andy."

The potluck. Oh, for fuck's sake. The neighborhood potluck kept slipping my mind. Who could blame me? I'd had a busy morning.

"Do you understand?" Don asked.

"Yes," I bobbed my head up and down.

"Good." When we reached the house, Don took me inside and made good on his promise to Kurt. I hadn't been sure that he was serious, but he was. He quickly located his favorite paddle, bent me over our dining room table, and made the spanking he'd given me in front of Chelsea seem like a happy game of patty-cake.

Don made sure to make my skin sizzle, and he only stopped when I was whimpering against the polished wood of the table. Then he picked me up and spread me out, making sure my asscheeks were slightly parted so I felt extremely exposed. He tickled my asshole as he licked my pussy until I couldn't even remember the pain from the spanking. Don's bristly goatee had me crying out each time he brushed his whiskers against my pussy. Then he sucked hard on my clit until I ground my cunt against his face and sobbed with pleasure.

I watched him lick my nectar off his lips, seeming to savor the taste.

"Spend the rest of the day preparing for the party," he said when he was finished, "I'll be home after work. Once everyone's set with food and drink, Andy and I will take care of you. And your needs." He didn't appear the slightest bit ruffled by our aerobically orotic morning. I was practically liquefied, and he simply got himself a glass of iced tea and then left for the office. I managed somehow to walk on my shaky legs to the bathroom and soak for an hour in a bubble bath. What was going to happen tonight? *How* would they take care of me?

I spent the rest of the day setting up the backyard—a gingham tablecloth on the picnic table. Big pitchers of lemonade and punch. Potato salad, food to grill, macaroni salad. Streamers from the tree branches. Thinking the entire time of Don and Andy. Of me and my needs. I would have made myself come if I had thought I could get away with it. But Don would be able to tell—I was certain. So I primped and I tidied, and I did my best not to close my eyes and imagine what was in store for me.

Don arrived home early and started the grill. By six o'clock our yard was filled with neighbors. I tried my best to make conversation, to be charming and witty and not constantly look to the door to see if Andy had arrived. As if to mentally torture me, Andy didn't show up until close to eight, but Chelsea did. She kept her eye on me, and Don introduced her to some of his kinkier friends. He seemed happy to see her, but he clearly wasn't going to get sidetracked. By the time Andy stepped into our yard, I was a mess of nerves, and my panties were so wet, I could have wrung them out with both hands.

I actually let out a huge sigh of relief when I caught sight of Andy's black leather jacket. He was there, right next to Don at the grill. I saw his short gray-black curls, his scruff of evening shadow.

Don didn't bother with any niceties. He didn't excuse himself from our guests. He simply motioned for me to follow him and he and Andy went back into the house.

What were they going to do to me? What was going to happen next?

I think I had a mini orgasm on my way down the hall. I felt as if my pleasure was made of knots on a string, being slowly unraveled one by one. When I opened the door to our upstairs bedroom, Don and Andy were waiting for me. The "World's Best Dad" had his belt off and Don had a pair of handcuffs in one of his big hands. God, they must have planned this. That's all I could think. Because Don didn't have to say a word to Andy, our neighbor simply cocked his head at me and waited.

I thought of all the times I'd been over to Andy's for coffee in the morning. Or to deliver a package that I'd signed for in his stead. I thought of caroling with him over the holidays, the time we'd all gone to snow country together. I saw the scar on the back of his hand that I knew he'd gotten when a jack had given out while he was changing the tire on his truck. I knew so much about him, but I didn't know him like this. I watched him snap the leather in his hand, and I felt weak. Don took pity on me. That is to say, he undressed me without making me do the work, and he bent me over our California King and told me to prepare myself.

"Andy treasured that mug," he said.

Stupid mug, I thought uselessly. Stupid Monday. When had I experienced a more brutal kickstart to the week? Then Don did something mean. He touched my pussy and I let out a dangerously sexy moan. He had found me out. I was wetter than ever. He swiped his fingertips over my own lips, and he grabbed me by the chin and looked me directly in the eye.

"Taste your honey," he demanded. I flicked tho tip of my tongue out and I licked my juices off my lips. "If you're telling yourself that you don't need this, that you don't want this, then you're lying to yourself."

I sighed. He was right. All the games he plays. All the ways he dominates and humiliates me. I love him for every last one. That didn't make holding myself still while Andy whipped me any easier to bear. I locked my arms and did my best, but after ten blows, I failed and brought one hand back to cover my smarting hindquarters. Don was on me quickly. He had my wrists bound in those cuffs and he looped the chain over the hook anchored at the top of our bed. I wasn't going anywhere now, and I most definitely wasn't going to be able to cover my bottom, a fact that didn't escape Don. He said to Andy, "Ten more, I think, and then you can take her ass."

Oh, god. Oh fuck. Oh, god.

I didn't even feel the next ten strokes. All I could think of was what Don had just said. *Ten more and you can take her ass.* My ass. Andy, handsome hunky Andy, was going to fuck my ass. I closed my eyes tight and wondered whether I might be dreaming. Perhaps the whole fucking day had been a dream. But then Andy dropped the belt—I heard the sound of the buckle hitting the floor—

and that clank was too real to have been in any dream of mine.

Don said, "Lube her up," and I felt my cheeks being splayed and then a river of greasy lube being poured over my asshole. My pussy spasmed at the sensation. I groaned when Andy roughly pushed a thick finger into my ass, spreading a little lube in there as well. At my moan, our neighbor took a few seconds to callously finger-fuck me until I was whimpering. I wished my hands were free so I could hide my face, but Don wasn't having any of my bashfulness. He lightly slapped my cheek and said, "This is what happens to bad girls."

I saw that his dick was hard in his slacks. I found that my mouth was watering. I wanted to suck him. I wanted to show him what a good girl I could be if given a chance. I wasn't sure what the right thing—at least, the right thing according to Don—would be. But I took a risk and said, "May I blow you?"

He looked at Andy instead of me. I wondered why only for a second, and then I felt Andy push forward, spearing me with his cock. At that precise moment, Don unzipped his slacks and took out his baseball bat of a dick. I had wanted his cock all day and I'd been denied. Now, as Andy made himself comfortable in my ass, Don let me have at his dick. First, he smacked my cheeks with the head, and then he rested the tip on my full lower lip.

"Slowly," he said, "I want you to take your time. Make it last."

It wasn't easy to focus with Andy in my backdoor, but I did my best. I wanted to prove myself to my man. I wanted to win back some brownie points. Andy fucked me hard and fast, and Don used my mouth nice and slow. The two warring actions were difficult for me to comprehend, but I did my best. I held my body in check for Andy, and I let Don set the pace he desired with his cock in my mouth. I was sure he was going to shoot down my throat when he came, and I was surprised when he pulled back before reaching completion.

Andy had no such compulsion. He came in a pounding rush, pumping his load deep inside me, and then he pulled out and reached for his belt.

"She's not done making things up to you," Don said. "Not by a long shot."

Andy met my eyes in the mirror over our dresser, and he winked at me. "You know, I always hated that mug," he said. Then he was out the bedroom door, on his way to the party, and Don and I were alone.

"Is your ass hot?" he asked next.

"Yes, Don."

"We're going to keep it that way. Tomorrow morning, you're going to go over to Andy's house and ask him for a maintenance spanking. On your lunch break, Chelsea will give you another. And when you get home tomorrow, you'll get one from me."

If he touched my clit, I would come.

"Chelsea's really interested in helping me to train you properly. She has this thought that getting you to wear a clamp on your clit while you work will force you to focus better. I told her to give it a shot. Nothing ventured…right?"

He got behind me, and he slid his thick cock into my pussy. I gripped onto him tightly with my inner muscles, but Don wasn't really interested in fucking me like this. He was simply wetting his dick in my pond, getting himself ready to go where Andy had already been.

A few strokes, and he pulled out and pressed his cockhead to my asshole. I was so primed by Andy that I opened up for him with no resistance. He slid in easily, and then he was the one to moan. That sounds lit me up inside. Everything he'd done today—the entire way he'd orchestrated our sex life—had been for me. But this was for him. Fucking my dripping ass after our neighbor had come inside me, this was all for Don.

He held my hips and he ground forward, really working me hard. I was panting from the thrill of the ride, and I felt transported when Don reached one hand beneath me to strum my slippery clit. He always knows precisely how to touch me. When I need it rough, he hurts me. When I want gentle, he fulfills my needs with compassion. Now his fingers took me exactly where I needed to go, tugging my clit as if he was working a dick in his hand, and I knew we were going to climax together.

I didn't make a noise—remembering our guests in the yard. I bit my lip and pressed my face to the pillow, bucking back on Don as the sweetness floored me. He filled my ass with his come, and I thought of the fact that his load was mixing with Andy's, lubing his shaft and running down his balls. That dirty image gave me an extra rush, and my climax seemed to extend—to grow into something bigger.

"Oh, Don," I whispered into the pillow.

I was demolished by the time Don pulled out and wrapped me in his arms. He held me like that until I caught my breath, and then he undid the cuffs and rubbed my wrists lightly. I set my head against his chest and listened to the sound of his breathing. The noise soothed me after the tumultuous day I'd had. I found myself lazily tracing circles over his flat belly as I recalled the multitude of surprises my husband had delighted me with. First Chelsea, then Kurt, then Andy…

"Now clean yourself up and go join the potluck," Don said, stroking my hair. "I think Chelsea wants to have a few words with you back behind the garage."

Maybe I was wrong, I thought to myself as I head to the bathroom for a quick rinse. Maybe my luck hadn't run out after all.

I couldn't wait to see what Tuesday would bring. Fucking Tuesday.

KINKING THE CLASSICS

THE MAPLE OLD FASHIONED

The Maple Old Fashioned is for a conversational charmer, dashing arm candy, and a delicious cad behind closed doors. This simple, eloquent cocktail tastes like a memory of your morning fuck over brunch—with a kick.

An Old Fashioned is a whiskey cocktail standard, but this variation takes out the fluff of simple syrup and adds the sweet and down-low groove of maple syrup in its stead. Base your seduction on a straight-but-not-narrow bourbon, use real maple syrup, and tickle the mixture with bitters that are kinkier than your neighbors' old Angostura.

Ingredients

    2 shots of bourbon whiskey
    1/2 shot of maple syrup
    Sliver of lemon rind, 1"
    Dash of bitters
    Ice: one large square or ball

Instructions

Pour the maple syrup into your glass. Set the ice in, and add your bourbon in a bit at a time, stirring in slow circles between pours to ensure it mingles with the syrup on every level. Add a splash of bitters. Cut your sliver of lemon rind and slide the white side around the inside of the rim of the glass. Give it a twist, and slip it in. Give your bitters a little shake—a drop or two will do—and let the carousing begin.

THE PROFESSOR'S WIFE

BY AMELIA MONROE

I am married to an absent-minded professor. Pause for a moment and consider exactly what that means.

Because trust me, it's not as cute as it sounds.

Marcus is handsome—dark hair silvering early at the temples— as if his hair *knew* to go gray and create that distinguished intellectual air. He has a lean body usually clad in broadcloth oxfords and chinos. He wears tortoiseshell spectacles and always shaves with a cream and a boar's hair bristle shaving brush.

In order for his world to operate smoothly, I work loyally to make sure his shirts are ironed, his briefcase is where he wants it (if not where he left it), his wallet contains a suitable amount of money, his keys are on the hook by the door.

Marcus is made up of a variety of little idiosyncrasies that bind me to him, but he is the quintessential over-thinker. He possesses such a big brain—and big thoughts—that he manages to lose track of the simple items. Like his keys. Or his wife's libido.

After a decade of marriage, I decided I would help him find me again. "Thad's coming by on Sunday to help with the attic," I told Marcus one morning. He was already in his study, notes spread out on the table, jazz playing softly in the background. Marcus can't listen to any music when he works except jazz. That's his white noise. While he works, he plays Coltrane and Gillespie and Miles Davis. When he's relaxing, he plays experimental music. When we first got together, he described the genre as "orgiastic." I had to look up the word: wild, abandoned, riotous, frenetic. Marcus, my buttoned-up professor only came undone to jazz.

That was one of my first attractions to him.

He held up his coffee mug. "Help with what attic?" he asked without looking up at me.

"*The* attic," I repeated. *What* attic did he think I meant?

"Help what with the attic?" he asked. Several of his lecture notes were decorated with rings from the coffee mug. I could see that he was deep in thought. I've always respected his work, but I was at the end of my patience. And so was my pussy.

"Help fuck the daylights out of me in the attic," I said evenly.

"Ha ha," Marcus said. Not a laugh. Not even a pretend laugh. More of a, "Aren't you cunning? I'll deal with you later" laugh. And sure—in the past, Marcus has always made time for me. But it's been his time, on his schedule. I wanted more. I wanted uproarious, debauched, wanton.

I wanted orgiastic.

"Did you hear what I said?" I asked Marcus as I refilled up his cup.

"Sure," he sipped his coffee, never looking up at me. "Thad's coming to help you clean the skylights on Sunday."

It was par for the course. Whenever Marcus is in concentrating mode, he blocks out everything else, but I had a feeling he wouldn't be blocking out this for long.

Sunday arrived, and I put on a short cherry-printed sundress and went to show Thad around. He was a Chem Major from the university who had helped me out with odd jobs during the school year. He was patient, hardworking, and one of the most beautiful male specimens I'd ever laid eyes on. I'd seen the way he watched me when he thought I wasn't looking. I was about to put the chemistry I sensed between us into motion.

I didn't waste any time. When I showed him the attic, he looked around and said, "The place is fucking spotless. Oh, I'm sorry, Mrs. Daniels."

"Carla," I told him. "And don't apologize for saying fucking. Not in front of me. In fact, I've spent the past few weeks setting up for exactly that purpose." He looked blankly at me, so I continued. "Fucking."

In the center of the attic was a queen-sized mattress covered in leopard-print satin sheets. Gone were the boxes of who knows what. Even the dust bunnies had been given their hopping papers.

"What exactly did you want me to do?" he asked, and I saw him checking out my breasts.

"What do you think I want you to do?" I'd managed to find a second man who needed me to spell things out. Well, I was fine with that. I came toward him, and I was gratified that unlike Marcus he did not glaze over or misunderstand in any way. He said, "I don't know what you want me to do, but I know what *I* want to do."

Then he kissed me. Flames licked up and down my body. It had been long since I'd shared a first kiss. I felt as if I might liquefy in his embrace, but I wasn't ready for that to happen. Not yet.

"Hold that thought," I told him. "I need to get Marcus up here."

As I turned to go, Thad grabbed onto one of my wrists. "Tell me what you're planning," he insisted. So I did. Slowly. Carefully. Enunciating every word. To my delight, Thad was game.

"Marcus," I called down the stairs. "Can you help me out up here?"

"I thought you had Thad," he called back after a moment. I could hear the sound of jazz playing.

I motioned for Thad to come closer to me. I slid one hand into his pants and started to touch his cock. "I *do* have Thad," I yelled back. "I have his big hard cock in my hand."

There was a blast of happy notes as a horn player took a solo. I waited and then called down. "When he's done fucking me, he's going to fuck you."

The music abruptly went off.

I heard footsteps on the stairs. I hurried to push Thad down on the bed. Marcus moved faster than I expected. He was suddenly there, right by the bed, as I shifted aside my copper-colored panties and began to lower myself on Thad's glorious dick.

"What… what's going on?" Marcus asked.

I pushed my hips up and then slid down Thad's pole. "I'm fucking Thad," I said.

Marcus blinked behind his spectacles. "You are," he agreed. "You most definitely are." He looked at the college boy. Thad seemed to have lost his ability to speak, but Marcus appeared truly awake for the first time in years.

"What did you say before?" he asked.

"I said that I was going to fuck Thad…" I pushed up and rocked down again. "And then he's going to fuck you."

It was that part that seemed to have captured Marcus' attention.

He stared from me to Thad again, and then he surprised me. He reached over and unzipped my dress, then pulled the fruity print over my head and tossed the sundress aside.

He got as close as he possibly could to the two of us and watched as I leaned forward, dangling my breasts in front of Thad's handsome face. Thad was a smart boy: 800 on his Math SATS, A four-year scholarship. He didn't have to be told what to do next. He started licking my erect nipples, using his hands to bring one breast to his mouth while he softly stroked the other, then switching until my whole body felt as if I were being petted.

"Oh, fuck," Thad suddenly said, and I turned my head to see what Marcus was doing. Thrillingly, Marcus had gotten on the bed with us. He was behind me, and out of my range of view.

Luckily, when I'd cleaned the room, I'd positioned a large, antique mirror against one wall. Who knew which relative we'd inherited this thing from. Fanciful cupids danced in the curlicues of woodwork. They would have been shocked scarlet had their little eyes been real. Because when I glanced into the silvered reflection I saw Marcus between Thad's legs. Now, the boy's cock was in me. So what was Marcus up to?

"Oh, fucking fuck," Thad said. That was clearly the word of the day.

"What's he doing to you?" I whispered. I was desperate to know. I started frigging my clit as Thad said, "He's tonguing my balls."

"Holy hell," I sighed, imagining that, thinking of Marcus who never spoke out about any fantasy, who never seemed interested in much in bed. But now. Now he was on the mattress between college boy's thighs, and he was licking and lapping Thad's balls.

I remembered when Marcus and I had first met. How I'd waited until he was no longer my professor before I went for him. He'd been absentminded then, distracted, if you will. But I'd managed to get him to focus, at least momentarily. Now, with Thad's help, I'd done it again.

"Oh, he's lapping at them," Thad murmured.

Well, good for Marcus, I thought to myself.

"I need more," said Marcus. "I can't get where I want…"

I had a cure for that. I moved off Thad's cock and forward, until I was straddling the college senior's face. Thad didn't miss a trick. He used his fingers to spread my nether lips and he began to dine on my sopping pussy. Dear lord, he was divine. Those co-eds at his school were blessed. He didn't rush. He took his time licking in circles around my swollen clit, moving away and then close in, over and over until I felt as if I would never come, or as if I was already coming. I felt lost in that golden pleasure haze, so lost in fact that I forgot to be paying attention to Thad. That is, until he began moaning into my cunt.

I backed off a little and I said, "What's he doing to you now?"

"Oh, Christ, Mrs.…" Thad moaned.

"Carla," I reminded him.

"Mrs. Carla," Thad echoed, clearly confused, obviously obliterated by the pleasure.

"Tell me, Thad," I insisted.

"He's rimming my asshole. Your husband's tongue is up inside my ass. It's deep up there. I've never felt anything like that."

I climbed back on his face then, and I ground against his mouth until I came. I couldn't help myself. I was so turned on by his words, that I simply needed release. I pressed my split hard against the college boy, and Thad helped me out by sucking my clit with the perfect pressure and rhythm. But when I'd had mine, I moved away and assessed the situation.

Marcus had taken off his glasses and was tonguing Thad's hole, and Thad's eyes were closed in bliss. I decided to suck Thad's cock to get it nice and wet for Marcus. That was an honorable, wifely thing to do, wasn't it? I squirmed close to Marcus in a way that allowed me to bob on Thad's cock until he said, "No, wait... I don't want to come yet. Don't make me come yet." That was the impetus to change positions. Marcus stripped quickly, and then Thad got behind my husband and he used some of the lube I'd bought for the occasion. He really got Marcus's asshole all nice and greasy before he pressed his cockhead against the hole.

Marcus looked at me with wild naked eyes and I smiled at him and said, "It's okay, baby. It's all good."

I got on the bed with the men, and I started to jerk Marcus off while Thad fucked him. That worked for me for a few minutes, my fist around Marcus' shaft. His cock was wet with pre-come and my fingers glided easily up and down that silky skin.

But then I needed more. I managed to wriggle once more into a position so I could suck on Marcus, taking his cock into my mouth and bathing it in a nirvana of heat and wetness. Marcus began to fuck my face fiercely, unable to help himself. I'd never seen him lose control before. Never heard the type of moans he was making. Thad was working him at a steady clip, bucking deep inside Marcus' asshole, whispering words to him—"You're so tight, so god damn tight."

I remembered seeing Marcus in front of the class that first day. The way he had forgotten his glasses were on his head, and he'd dropped his notes, and he'd squinted at the auditorium audience as if unsure of why we were there.

What was up with this crazy professor, I'd wondered. And then he'd done this masterful thing. He'd put on a jazz record—right at the start of class. The music had poured through tho room. Everyone had grown still. He'd waited until the first song was over, and then turned off the stereo. When he'd begun to speak, he owned us.

It was majestic. The transformation.

So when Marcus pushed me away, and pulled forward—when he flipped the position and took Thad—I heard music in my head.

Thad looked demolished but willing. Marcus pinned him to the mattress and motioned for me to hand him the lube. He oiled up his own dick and the returned the favor to Thad, parting the college boy's cheeks, introducing Thad to being a receiver. I was as floored by this display as I'd been by the other. Watching Marcus fuck Thad was hotter than any porn I'd ever viewed.

I leaned back on the pillows and stroked myself while the men went at it. Thad came first, dampening the sheet below him with spurt after spurt of his cream. Marcus didn't spill a drop of his seed. He used the boy's ass as his decanter. And I came again, loud enough that I was sure our neighbors would hear my cries emanating from the open windows.

I'd done what I'd set out to do. I'd gotten Marcus' attention once more. I'd created a riff of orgiastic indulgence.

Now that the attic's clean, I'm going to ask Thad to come over next weekend to help me in the basement—*and* I'm going to see if he'll bring a friend. I'm pretty sure Marcus will play along.

GOOD HOUSEKEEPING

TIPS FOR HOUSEHOLD BONDAGE

There is an occasion now and again where someone requires restraint. On these occasions, when we've got a fever to see our lover in a bind, it pays to keep a few happy housewife (and househusband) tips in mind.

Agree beforehand what you both want, and don't want, from a bit 'o bondage around the chateau; double check that you've got clear agreement that you both want to all manner of wicked, wonderful, filthy, and deviously delightful things to each other. Make sure that everything regarding your mutual decisions to tie, bind, spank, lick, suck and fuck is all clear as crystal, with no deviations (unless they beg sweetly). Establish a safeword in case one of you needs a powder break when things get intense.

TO HAVE AND TO HOLD

   * Stretchy, silky materials found in pantyhose, silk scarves, and neckties can tighten down knots in ways that might become painful or impossible to untie. Be prepared to cut them off if needed.

   * Try to plan ahead by stashing proper rope, cuffs, or bondage accessories around the kitchen, study, or foyer for stellar surprises.

* Don't lay your bound bounty on tied-up or cuffed wrists: this can injure.

* Not all kitchen chairs, tables or living room furniture can hold up under a bondage romp: test first so you don't have a mishap!

* If you're not sure your knots will hold, or the Chicago chairs can stay put, erotically command your lover to stay in bondage.

HOME SWEET HOME

BY TASHA WATERS

Home Sweet Home.

Here I am. On my knees. Again.

I'm waiting. I'm kneeling. I can feel the raised edges of the needlepoint letters pressing into my naked skin.

When I originally embroidered the pillow, my thoughts were consumed by the hues. A pink pearl embroidery thread for the lettering. Scarlet roses growing in emerald grass. I spent hours on the handiwork—cross-stitch, satin stitch—because I had hours to spend. My husband is an executive who provides the best of everything I could ever ask for. Most women would think my life is a dream come true. I don't clean our house because we employ a maid service. I'm not required to cook because we have a gourmet chef. A gardening team tends to our landscaping. The high-end grocery store delivers.

I would say I'm not complaining, except I am.

What do I do? I am crafty. Because you can't hire someone to be crafty for you. And I'm crafty in more ways than one.

My love of cross-stitching is what led to my current submissive position: kneeling on the *Home Sweet Home* pillow. I'm entirely nude, my asshole greased and fitted with a curving, jeweled metal butt plug, my plump lips opened around an exquisite ball gag fitted neatly into place, silk blindfold over my lids.

Della stands behind me, my leash in her hand, my special collar satisfyingly snug around my throat. We're waiting for Raymond to arrive because Della decided that today's the day to go public with what I'd been keeping a secret for far too long. I am Della's pet all day, every day, as soon as Ray leaves for work. Up until now, Della has been forced to leave me unmarked by cocktail hour. Now she wants to go further and for that we need to bring my husband into the deal.

The door opens. I hear his standard, "Honey-baby?" call from the hall, and I know he will be dropping his keys into the ceramic bowl we bought on our last trip to Santa Fe, leaving his coat on the antique walnut rack, walking along the black-and-white marble hallway to find…

Me.

Here I am. In the middle of our spacious living room. Waiting.

I hear the sharp sound of him sucking in his breath, and then I hear Della say, "Raymond. I've got your drink all mixed and ready. Would you care to have a seat? There's something I'd like to talk to you about."

Raymond doesn't say a word. This isn't surprising. My husband is a deep thinker; he chooses his statements carefully. I know he's processing what he's seeing, and I hear him down a big swallow of the chilled martini Della mixed for him.

"I'm not sure how well you know your wife," is how Della starts. I wonder how Raymond will process that bit of news. "See, the girl is a filthy little fuck-slut. A come-whore. A drippy, sodden plaything who requires all sorts of devious attention paid to her pussy. And her nipples. And her asshole. She likes to serve. In fact, I'd say she *needs* to serve. For the past six months, she's been serving me."

Raymond is still silent. I can imagine him looking at me. Taking in my appearance. He's never seen me like this. Not even close to this. Not even on Halloween or Mardi Gras or costume events. I am naked before him in every possible way.

Accept me, I beg internally. *Love me.*

Della continues, "Sometimes, I put clamps on her nipples and tug on the chain until she cries. Sometimes I use a special vibrator right on her clit, and I don't take the toy away even after she comes. It's torture, but she likes that. The thing is, what I haven't been able to do is leave a mark."

"Jesus," says Raymond softly. We have never done anything kinky together. In our four-year marriage, we've only ever fucked in the dark. This has always confused me. Here we live in paradise. He could have taken me outside, by the reflecting pond. He could have screwed me in our mirrored dining room or in the massive shower with the four big heads. Instead, he has treated me like one of his treasured *objets d'art*. With kid gloves. With reverence. But never the way I want.

"What do you think about the way she looks?"

Raymond doesn't seem to have an answer to that. At least, not right away. I hear the sound of his glass being set on the coffee table. I hear him walking around me.

"She looks..." he starts, "she looks..." he tries again, "she looks so fucking sexy." His voice is hoarse.

I sag with relief, that is, until Della continues: "Did you know she likes anal sex?"

Raymond seems to realize he's supposed to respond, because he clears his throat and says, "No. We've never done that."

"You might not have done that. But she has. Oh, has she ever. One thing I like to do is bind her on her stomach with her legs apart. I get behind her and I use rivers of lube between her asscheeks. Whole bottles of lube. I get her so greased up she's like this oiled-up buttercup. A flower with petals to peel open. And then I play with her asshole. Do you know what I mean?"

Raymond clears his throat again. He says, "I can guess."

"Can you? Would you like to? Or would you like me to describe how I play with your wife's backdoor?"

"Yes," he says. "Yes, I would. But I think I need another martini first."

I wish I could take the blindfold off to see Raymond's expression. Well, part of me wishes that. Part of me is supremely grateful that I am in the dark. Not that I had believed Raymond would be violent. But you never know how a person will react to unexpected news, and this is definitely unexpected.

As Della mixes a fresh drink, I think about the series of events that brought me to this place.

Up until I'd met Della, I'd been the perfect wife. The type you sometimes see and think—damn, doesn't that woman ever have a hair out place? With me, the answer would have been no. Because I had all the time in the world to make sure every hair was perfectly *in* place. I had hours to spend at the salon, at Pilates, at yoga, at the gym. I had hours to spend trying on shoes, pouring my body into skin-tight designer dresses, going out to lunch with lady friends who never ate a bite. Ladies who lunch is a misnomer. They should be called ladies who push their lunch around on their plates and gossip about fucking the gardener.

I'd been bored out of my ever-loving skull. Della had shown me a whole new way to behave. She had awakened me from the somnambulant state that had become my life. What thirty-two year old woman really wants to spend her hours engaged in handlwork?

Raymond hadn't seen the cross-stitches I'd made in my boredom. *Fuck This Shit. I'm So Over This. I Hate My Life*. Della had saved me. We'd run into each other one afternoon at the craft store. I was surprised to see her there, since she seemed like such a modern woman. She wore all black, scraped her white-blonde hair off her face in a severe style, drove the type of mint-conditioned European sports car that shone so bright it seemed as if she must get the thing detailed every day.

What was she doing at Hortense's Hobbies?

"Getting some rhinestones to bling up a pair of handcuffs," was what she told me. My pussy had responded before I could, growing wet in my dainty yellow panties.

"Handcuffs?" I'd asked her, tentatively.

"They're a gift," she'd said.

Should I have been surprised when she showed up the next day with the handcuffs for me? She'd known, she said, that I was home alone. She'd sensed, she explained, watching me in the garden, staring into space, aimlessly doing nothing… she'd found me. And so in between meetings, on days when she could get away from the office, whenever she was able to spare an hour, I was her pet.

In fact, I was *always* her pet, even when she wasn't there.

Sometimes, she left me tied to her bed while she went to work. Sometimes she had me nap in a basket in her laundry room, a rhinestone-studded collar with a little bell around my neck.

She strokes me now as she tells Raymond this. She strokes my hair and calls me a good girl and twists the plug in my ass until I cry out around the gag.

Then she says, "Your wife has the most sensitive little asshole. I was charmed when I discovered I could actually make her come by playing with her backdoor alone. No clit stimulation at all. What I like to do, though, is put a clamp on her clit and then fuck her ass with a big, fat vibrator. Then sometimes, I squat over her and let her rim me while I turn that vibrator on high. She cries when she comes. Did you know that? Tears streak her cheeks when the pleasure becomes too much for her."

I hear the sound of Raymond draining his second martini. Then he bends down next to me. I can smell his aftershave, can feel his closeness.

"Touch her pussy," Della said. "She's dripping. I haven't let her come all day. She's been waiting for you."

Will he? Will he do what our neighbor instructs? Raymond had always referred to Della as "the ice queen," observing that it was no surprise she was unmarried. Who'd put up with a woman that cold?

Now he seems as captivated as I am, because I feel his fingertips probing my pussy, and he groans at the wetness awaiting him.

"See that?" Della says. "Do you need more proof than that of your wife's innate submissiveness?"

"No," Raymond responds. "No, I don't."

He touches my pussy again, his fingers stroking, and I shiver all over and do my very best not to come on his hand. I don't know what Della will do or say if I climax without her permission.

"Now, Raymond," Della says, "What I'm proposing is a deal."

"A deal," he echoes, vaguely, in a daze.

"You get her at night, like you always do. I get her in the day."

Raymond laughs, surprising me. "I don't get her at night," he says. "I mean, sometimes we have sex at night, but I don't think I've ever understood her. We've been together for years, and I had no idea…why wouldn't she tell me?" Then directly to me, "Why didn't you tell me this is what you wanted?"

I can't answer. Not with the big gag in my mouth. Della speaks for me.

"She didn't know."

"How could she not know?"

"People keep their fantasies buckled down deep. She didn't know she was sub until I showed her. But you know you're dominant, don't you?"

Holy fuck. My heart's racing. Raymond is a Dom?

He pinches my clit then, almost absentmindedly, and says, "My fantasies run that way. Yes."

"Of course they do. You'd already made her your pet. She was in a prison."

"I give her everything." Raymond stands up. I can imagine him full height, looking at Della. They'd be eye to eye, both about six feet tall.

"You gave her nothing that she wanted. She had no purpose. Someone did everything for her. That's not a life."

"And this is?" I'm tugged suddenly forward. Raymond has apparently taken up my leash.

"Oh yes," Della says. "And you know it. You wanted her like this from the start. I had to show her…and now I'm showing you. I get her in the day—when my schedule permits—you get her at night. All night. Every night."

"Do you want this?" Raymond asks, and I can tell he's talking to me now. I nod vigorously and try not to drool too obviously around the gag.

What comes next is what I have always wanted. What comes next is that Raymond carries me to the bedroom. Raymond starts, spanking me because I lied to him—omission, he says, is the same as lying. He spanks me with his hand and his belt, and then he makes me rim Della while he fucks my asshole with the plug, pulling it out and pushing it back in while I drive my tongue between Della's pearly cheeks.

He fucks my asshole with that plug until I am desperate to feel something bigger there, something harder, something real. But before he takes my ass, he spanks my pussy. Della's never done this. Nobody has ever done this. He has me lie on my back, and he has Della hold my thighs apart, so that I don't flinch, so that I don't close my legs. With his fingers held in a stiff row, he spanks my pussy until I come. I am a slippery, wet mess by the time he stops. I am gone, over the rainbow, behind the gym, through the looking glass. Raymond spanks my pussy as he tells me that he will be punishing me every night, from now on. That he will put ice on my clit when I'm bad. That he will put clamps on my nipples and tighten the screws. That he will carve a knob of expensive ginger and fig me before he canes me. I come more times than I can count. And then Raymond pulls off the blindfold, has Della undo my gag, and he fucks my mouth.

I get him wet. I know what's going to happen next. But I don't know how good it's going to feel. Raymond has me on my back, and he puts my legs up. Della holds my asshole open for my husband as he slots the head of his cock right up with my hole. He tells Della, "Pinch her clit while I fuck her ass. Pinch the bad girl's clit nice and hard."

It's like I never stop coming.

Nothing has ever felt this sweet before.

We spend all night lost in debauchery, doing the deeds that I dreamed of. That I fantasized about. That I jerked off to in the garden. In the garage. In the shower.

Tomorrow I will start on a new needlepoint. I'm going to do *Home Sweet Home* again.

But this time, I'm going to mean it.

KINKING THE CLASSICS

THE VERY DIRTY MARTINI

A perfect dirty martini is like good porn: Everyone makes martinis, but no matter if they're using top or bottom shelf spirits, hardly anyone gets it right. But when it's right, it feels better at first taste than slipping into cool silk panties on a hot summer night—it's like slipping out of them for a really good reason.

The classic martini is made with gin, which lends the martini a distinctive lilt on the palate; if you want to highlight your martini's exquisite filthiness from the first lick forward, a top-shelf vodka is your best friend. Ordering a dirty martini means you'll get the usual with a splash of olive juice, but filthiness comes in degrees. Like life, your martini should be as filthy as you dare. Place your vodka in the freezer for flawless execution.

Ingredients

    2 1/2 shots of ice-cold vodka
    1/2 shot dry vermouth
    4 teaspoons olive brine; more as you like it

Instructions

Grab your shaker, and get it ready—fill it almost to the brim with ice. Everything wet goes in your shaker; vodka, vermouth and brine. Shake for around ten seconds; shaking adds air bubbles, which gives it cloudiness and freshens the taste. Swirl enough vermouth in each glass to give it a caress, then pour your libidinous libation through a strainer and add your olives. If it's not dirty enough, you know what to do.

PICTURE PERFECT

BY EMILIE PARIS

Hunter and I were in a sweaty sixty-nine when his phone rang. I wasn't sure if he was going to answer. I knew *I* couldn't. My lips were wrapped around that big, fat dick of his. Anyway, why would he want to talk on the phone? What if it was a sales call? Or a work disaster? Surprisingly, he untangled one arm and reached for his cell. I felt his breath on my wet pussy as he spoke, and then I heard the unmistakabe click as he took a picture.

"Hey!" I squealed, scrambling around on the mattress. "What are you doing?"

"Mark wanted a photo."

"Of my pussy?"

"Yeah." His blue-green eyes glimmered in the light. "He wants more, too."

I'd flipped around and was now nestled between his tan, muscular thighs. "What sort of pictures?" I asked, staring at his cock rather than his face.

"You bob that pretty head of yours up and down my dick, and we'll see if we can't make a movie for Mark."

I was so horny from Hunter's tongue on my split that I didn't even pause. I started sucking him again, posing this time so he could aim his camera-phone and shoot me engaged in this succulent act. I realized that the filming was turning me on. I'd never been in a dirty video before, and let's just say I wasn't planning on joining the PTA in this lifetime. I put more effort into the blowjob than I had before, basking in the knowledge that Mark was going to see me in this most personal act.

After about thirty seconds, Hunter stopped filming and told me he was sending the evidence. So aroused, I climbed onboard his cock and started to ride the slicked-up, juicy pole. In this position, I found myself staring at myself in the mirror over Hunter's bed. I'd been with Lorna when she bought the mirror at an antique store in the city. She'd been hesitant to splurge—the price was astonishing—but now I was extremely glad she had.

I tilted my head, taking in the way I looked riding my husband's best friend—and my best friend's husband. Honestly? I looked good. My long black hair flicked this way and that. My short cranberry-dyed bangs bounced when I bounced, and then fluttered back into place. I'd been wearing a dark scarlet lipstick when we'd started, but much of the color had faded during my adventurous blowjob.

I cupped my tits in my hands and squeezed then pinched my own nipples and arched my back. I was a porn star. I was a kink queen.

Hunter's phone rang again.

"Really?" I said, in a sarcastic way. "What do you think he wants now?"

"You answer," Hunter said. "He's your husband, after all."

I grabbed the phone and pressed the button. It wasn't Mark, though. It was Lorna, Hunter's wife, and she said, "Hey, Stella. Tell me what you're doing. I miss you."

I knew what she meant. She meant that she missed the visual. Hunter, Mark, Lorna, and I tend to play together. All in one room. This was the first time we'd tried swapping partners entirely. Clearly, my husband and Hunter's wife wanted to keep the connection going even though we were in different houses.

"I'll tell you," I said to her in a soft voice, "if you tell me."

"Well, your handsome man is fucking my ass," she said, "really good and slow. He got me all riled up with his tongue first. You know how good he is at rimming. I love when he sticks his tongue up inside me."

I put Lorna on speaker, so Hunter could hear her, too.

"Then he got out the industrial bottle of lube you guys keep by the bed—*perverts*—and he oiled me up good and proper."

I could feel Hunter's cock getting even harder inside me. The sound of his wife's sultry voice was definitely working him up.

"He went nice and slow, exactly how I like it. Just the head at first while he strummed his fingers on my clit to get me accustomed to the sensation. It wasn't until I was begging him to pound me hard did he give me the full package. Your man really likes to go deep."

I felt my cheeks flushing at her story and my heart beating even faster. Lorna's tale made me want anal, too. But I wanted something more. "I want to see," I said, not satisfied with hearing about the story or exchanging photos. "Show me."

That's how we ended up on FaceTime, truly breaking the barrier separating us.

"What did we miss?" Lorna asked me. I held the phone and looked at her shining face. She was breathing hard. Mark had clearly put her through a workout. So far, Hunter and I had sixty-nined and done a little missionary before cleaning each other up again. We hadn't gone in for anything seriously kinky. Sounded like Mark and Lorna had us beat on that front. I told her the deal, and she started to stroke herself, obviously growing aroused on my words.

"He showed me your harness and your dildo," Lorna continued. "Before we're done tonight, I'm going to strap that thing on and take his ass. Seems only fair."

Oh, man. That did me in. The thought of petite, blonde Lorna buckling into my leather harness and reaming Mark with my powder-blue dildo made me come. I really let loose, moaning and sighing. Having an audience amped up my pleasure in ways I wasn't initially prepared for.

Hunter grabbed the phone and said, "You just made your best friend come like a powerhouse, baby. She's squeezing my dick like there's no tomorrow. God, it's fucking amazing."

He made sure to point the camera at our junction, so Lorna could see for herself. Then he set the phone down and flipped me on the bed. For a few moments, the four of us were lost. I heard the sound of Lorna coming, and I heard Mark whisper to her that he was going to rinse off and come back for more. Hunter didn't mind the lull in the conversation. He focused his attention on me. "You want me in your ass now, don't you, pretty?"

"Oh, yes, Hunter."

He started to simply fondle my ass then, cradling my rear cheeks, kissing them. I closed my eyes as he devoted himself to my ass. His fingers stroked me, and then he parted my cheeks and kissed my hole. I half-sighed half-moaned at the pleasure. Hunter paused and said, "Tell me, Stella. Tell me everything."

I picked up the phone to see who was watching now, and there was Mark, wet from a dip in the shower, a blue towel around his taut physique. Hunter amended his statement. "I mean, tell Mark."

"Hey, baby," I said, as Hunter began to oil up my back door. "I..." Hunter's thick fingers slowly opened me up, and I found it difficult to speak. Lorna was practically a phone sex worker with her sultry purr. But I was struggling simply making words come out in English.

"Tell him," Hunter insisted from behind me.

"Hunter's going to fuck my ass," I said to Mark.

"Oh, yeah?" my man said. "And do you want him to?" His eyes told me he already knew the answer to that question. I found looking at him while Hunter was prepping me even sexier than what we'd done before—by ourselves. This added facet of arousal was almost too erotic for me to handle. Behind Mark, I saw our wedding photo on the nightstand. Didn't we look beautiful in that picture, proper and fancy in our expensive outfits? Now, we were stripped down to our basest level—but in my opinion, we looked even better.

"Do you?" Mark demanded.

"Yes, baby."

"More than that, Stella," Mark said. "I want to hear all about it. Don't hold back."

Hunter wasn't holding back—that's for sure. He had slid his thick finger in my rear hole and he was plunging the digit in and out of me at a deliriously slow, sensual pace. I handed the phone back to my lover, set my head on the mattress and sighed. My pussy felt as if it was opening up like a hothouse flower. I was so turned on I couldn't think straight.

"Tell him," Hunter demanded.

"He's finger-fucking my asshole," I told my husband. "He's getting me ready."

"I can see," Mark said, and a tremor worked through me. He was watching, as if he was with us in the bedroom. He was watching his oldest friend in the world touching me in the most intimate way. Hunter handed me back the phone, and I could just imagine how I must look to my husband. It was hard not to simply melt into the mattress. Hunter kept touching my rear opening, and I thought I might actually be able to come from anal stimulation alone. That had never happened to me before, but that didn't mean it couldn't. There's always a first time.

"You ready for that big dick of his, right?" Mark asked.

"Yeah," I whispered.

"You like his cock in your tiny hole, don't you?"

"Oh, fuck yeah," I sighed.

"You're such a dirty girl," Mark said. "You do know what this means, don't you?"

I did, and I said, "You're going to spank me when we swap back."

That's what always happened. Whenever we played with our friends, Mark would punish me afterward. He would spank me for liking it. He would fuck all my holes for being insatiable. It was one of my favorite parts of our deal.

"You can count on that," Mark agreed. "When you get home, I'm going to bend you over my lap and give your bottom the hardest spanking ever with your favorite paddle. I know you need a good, solid punishment after a swap, don't you, baby? Just to show you how much I care."

"Yes, Mark." His words were pure passion to me, aural foreplay. And then there was Hunter, pressing the head of his cock against my asshole. I felt him dribble a few more drops of lube at the junction where we were joined, oiling me up with lusty exuberance.

"Tell Mark to give Lorna a spanking for me," Hunter said as he rocked his hips forward and thrust inside me.

I babbled something unintelligible into the phone.

"Do it," Hunter insisted.

"Hunter wants you to spank Lorna," I said, panting.

"Give me the phone," my lover commanded. I scooted the cell back towards him on the mattress and crumpled in relief. I didn't have to talk anymore. I could bask in the feeling of being filled back there by Hunter's thick cock. I started to rub my clit with two fingers, building up to my climax. Being filled in my ass was sublime. Having my husband know the score was even better. The fact that Mark was now about to punish my girlfriend was incendiary.

A woman can only take so much.

I heard Hunter say into the phone, "Put her over your lap, man, and give her a real spanking. I want to see her red asscheeks when I fuck her tonight. And hey, Mark? Spank her pussy a little bit, too. She needs it like that. Can you angle the camera so Stella can see?"

For a moment, I forgot about what Hunter was doing to me, and that's saying something, because Hunter is equipped with a powerful rod. Mark positioned Lorna over his lap and he started to spank her. I don't think I'd ever seen anything so sexy before. My comely girlfriend was being punished by my husband. He wasn't holding back, either. He was using that paddle like the pro he is, and in moments, she was moaning and arching her back. I was impressed that Mark was able to work both the camera and the paddle with such finesse. But he didn't seem to have a problem being an amateur x-rated cinematographer.

I hadn't known that Lorna was into being spanked. Somehow, this tidbit of information had escaped me. I'd never thought to confess my own spanking desires to her. But now I realized we were more alike than I'd thought.

"Her pussy," Hunter reminded him.

"Yes, her pussy," Mark echoed. Then Lorna was being positioned on my bed. I saw the stack of books on my nightstand—mysteries and vintage detective fiction. I saw the candy pink satin sheets I'd bought on sale the week before, and I saw that Lorna was leaving a wet spot on them. Mark placed her as he wanted her and then put her own hands on her thighs. "Keep yourself open wide like that for me," he instructed. He took an artsy shot of her short blonde pubes, and he tugged them and made Lorna moan. She had a tiny tattoo of a four-leaf clover to the right of her navel. I wondered if Hunter liked to make a wish when he touched it.

Mark and the camera went to our closet, and I saw that he was giving me a close-up of our decadent devices, as if he were inviting me into the decision of which one to choose for Lorna. I wasn't surprised when he landed on a lavender suede flogger—one of my favorites.

He dangled the fronds in front of the phone, and then he dangled them in front of Lorna. She groaned and arched her back, and she spread her thighs even wider apart. It was clear to both of us that she was desperate for him to take care of her.

"You like your pussy spanked?" Mark asked.

Lorna and I said "yes" together. The men laughed, and Hunter, who was still working his big dick in and out of my tight asshole said, "You wait, kid. You'll get yours."

Mark handed Lorna the phone, and I was suddenly staring at my husband as he brought his wrist back and then let the suede flogger kiss Lorna's swollen pussy lips. She groaned and muttered something under her breath and Mark struck again. I came when he nailed her the third time. I wasn't even expecting the climax to happen. It was like a champagne bottle rocketing off. In a rush, the pleasure flooded through me, and I dropped the phone and ground my hips against Hunter, taking control of the ride for a moment. He didn't seem to mind. He let my inner muscles work him as my hips banged against his body.

"Your ass is so sweet and tight, Stella," he said. "I love fucking your backdoor."

The climax was intense, sparking a small series of orgasms that flared through me. Nearly delirious with pleasure, I continued pressing back to meet each thrust. "You love it, too," he murmured at my motions. "You like having my dick in your asshole."

"Yes," I told him. "Yes, I love it." The words were a breathless rush. I was going to come again if he kept talking to me like that. Or maybe I was simply never going to stop coming. I'd reached the highest pleasure plateau ever. I wanted to stay there. Hunter held my waist and drove his way toward his own finish line. I caught sight of the action on the phone again. Lorna was propped up by my throw pillows, and Mark was stroking her clit with the tip of his cock. He wasn't entering her. He was simply pushing his dickhead against her button over and over.

"Fuck me," she started begging. "Just fuck me!"

Hunter lifted the phone from the mattress and angled it behind me.

"And just think, when you get home, Mark's going to paddle this ass until your cheeks are all nice and hot." Hunter palmed my bottom as he spoke. "I bet that'll make you come, won't it?"

Jesus, he wasn't going to quit, was he? He was going to get me off again. He seemed to be thinking the same thing, because he started to play with my clit while he spoke. "And then he'll fuck you, won't he?"

"Yes, Hunter."

"Pussy or asshole?"

"Probably both."

"Lucky girl."

I pinched my clit then as Hunter filled me up, thinking yes, I was a very lucky girl indeed.

"And you know what?" Hunter asked as I came. "We'll be watching every fucking second.

GOOD HOUSEKEEPING

TIPS FOR KITCHEN SPANKINGS

The threshold for mixing pleasure with pain in a kitchen setting can be crossed in a variety of savory ways. Like a dash of bitters in a sweet drink, we're using swats to sweeten sex, not to dampen it; always start with a light application, no matter how naughty they're behaving. Heat them up between swats with erotic caresses, kisses, dirty words of encouragement, or a taste of oral sex. Give your kitchen quarry almost what they want… and then a little bit more.

Position your squirming plaything accordingly. Pull out a kitchen chair and push them ass over teakettle onto your lap. Or, they should assume the position with hands solidly on the kitchen sink's rim. Especially naughty beasties go all-fours on the cool floor tiles; have them hold a wooden spoon between the teeth as a further act of filthiness.

Choose smart implements; begin with a slow rhythm and build up gradually.

* Hands are sublime, but know that they'll get pained and tired quickly.

* Wooden spoons have allure, but they're extremely painful. Use with caution.

* The thinner and harder the implement, the meaner the bite. Metal is cruel.

* The end of any item will sting the worst.

* Never strike bony areas or the lower back.

* A wide surface on your implement will spread the impact, and let you spank them longer.

* Don't forget to caress and tap-tap-tap your spatula on eager genitals, too.

NEIGHBORHOOD WIVES WATCH

BY JEWEL RODRIGUEZ

"You're not supposed to be here," I hissed at Max.

What I wanted to say was, *"What the fuck? What are you doing here? Are you trying to ruin everything?"* I couldn't believe him. I had reminded him that morning about the party. I'd called him at lunch just to reiterate. I had even texted him. DON'T FORGET. GIRLS ONLY TONIGHT.

He'd promised he wouldn't come home until I called.

"Oh, shit," he said, looking extremely sheepish. "Things got so busy at work today. I totally forgot."

My cheeks flamed. I'd spent all day getting ready. I'd visited the florist for bouquets of fresh flowers—black-purple tulips that I'd arranged in art nouveau vases. I'd ordered platters of *hors d'ouevres* from the fancy gourmet store on the corner. Not since sorority rush had I tried so hard to get a group of ladies to like me. I had desperately wanted this to go well.

And now Max was ruining everything.

Max and I had only moved into the exclusive neighborhood a few months before. So I'd been shocked and quite honestly honored to be asked to host a Neighborhood Wives Watch meeting. I hadn't made many friends yet. I knew who the other women were, but we hadn't bonded. Tammy, the president of the group, had explained over the phone that the women got more done without the men. We were the ones who were watching, anyway. Of the five of us, not one went to an out-of-the-house job.

So when Max showed up like that before I'd even poured the white wine, I felt mortified. How could I be expected to watch what was going on in the neighborhood if I couldn't keep control of the comings-and-goings in my own house?

With all eyes on him, he checked his watch and stammered, "I didn't realize…"

"You didn't realize that you'd ignored what your wife told you?" Tammy sneered at him. I turned to look at her, surprised by her tone.

"You didn't realize that if you came to the meeting, you'd have to dress like a lady?" asked Betsey. My head swiveled in her direction. I felt as if I were watching a tennis match, one in which Max was the ball.

"You didn't realize that we were going to strip you down and use your cock for our own pleasure?"

Max's face showed his emotions clearly. He seemed as shocked as I was—but he also looked interested. What man wouldn't be? Four women were eying him as if he were the best bit of beefcake they'd ever seen.

"If you want to stay," said Tammy, "you'll have to pay the price."

"The price," Max echoed. I looked at him standing there still holding onto his charcoal-colored coat. He seemed confused, as if moving in any way might make us all dissolve into a dream, as if he didn't want that to happen. Betsey stood up and took the coat from him. She led him to the sofa, and had him sit between Lauren and Donatella.

Lauren stroked his cheek softly, and Max's eyes grew wider and wilder.

"He needs a shave," she told Betsey.

"Of course he does," Betsey said. "All over that sweet sexy body of his."

Max made a little guttural moan.

"See, we've been watching you, Sweetie," Betsey said to Max. "When you mow the lawn on the weekends wearing nothing but those shorts slung low on your hips, we're all a-drool. You've got a great body. Shame to keep it hidden under those suits for ten hours a day. Especially, this part."

Max moaned again. I looked and saw that Donatella was stroking his cock through his slacks. She did this in the same clinical way that Lauren had stroked his cheek.

"He's got such a nice package," Donatella said to Tammy. "And he's hard."

I found that I kept opening and closing my mouth, but no words were coming out. Betsey said my name then.

"Trish?"

She spoke my name a second time, putting a little more force behind the word. I looked at her in a daze. I couldn't compute the fact that these women were discussing my husband with as much detachment as if they'd been ordering a particular piece of steak at the local butcher.

Betsey took me into the kitchen and kindly poured me a glass of my own cooking sherry.

"I know you're new here," she said as I gratefully downed the drink. "So you don't know exactly how this works."

"How it *works*? How *what* works?"

"Well, as you know, we wives are all part of a Neighborhood Wives Watch club. And we like to watch each other…take care of each other's husbands if you know what I mean. We weren't sure how you'd feel about that. But clearly, Max is into the concept."

"What's the concept?" I needed her to spell it out. I needed to drink the Spanish sherry straight from tho burgundy-lıued bottle.

"We turn him into a sissy maid." She said the words as if I were a little slow, as if I should have cottoned on by then.

"All of your husbands?"

"Oh, yes. For different periods of time, you know. Tammy runs the tightest ship. Bruce is her full-time sub. As soon as he gets home from work, she has him stripped down to nothing but high heels and embarrassing little crotchless panties." Betsey giggled and shook her head. "Really. *Crotchless panties.* I have no idea where she found those. I guess you can order anything online these days. He does all the laundry, the cleaning, the shopping. If he's bad, she punishes him in the most dreamy ways. Her favorite is this chastity belt she locks him in. Oh, you should hear him beg her to let him free. He promises all sorts of things." Her eyes glowed, and then added, "Of course, if he's good, she allows him to eat her out."

"How do you know all that?"

"The cameras…"

I blinked at her, and then decided not to ask any more about Bruce. We could return to him later. "And your husband?" I asked.

"Dominic had a difficult time with the concept at first," she admitted. "He's in the mechanics industry, and he hangs out with these butch guys all day long talking about lug nuts and wrenches.

When I first shaved him completely bare, he kept saying 'What would the guys think?' But he learned that he really loves wearing flowery dresses. Especially with a girdle, and all kinds of foundation garments. You know that kind of old-fashioned touch."

I'd met Dominic and the thought of his big burly body in a floral dress almost made me bark laughter, but it was right then that I heard Max make a noise in the other room. I hurried back into the living room to see that in my absence, the remaining women had stripped him of his clothes and were inspecting him from all angles. Tammy pushed him over our coffee table and spread his asscheeks apart while I watched. She tapped her fingertip directly on his anus, and Max grunted and humped his hips against the table's edge.

"Let me…" Lauren said, and while I watched she took over from Tammy and got behind Max. To my utter shock, she started to actually rim my husband.

For a second, I thought I might pass out. Betsey put her arms around me, holding me steady.

"None of that," Tammy said to Max. "You get your pleasure when I say so." She pushed Lauren away, but had him stay like that while she started to spank him. I felt my breath quicken. Max had never looked so confused before, but I could tell that he was enjoying what was happening. Betsey ran a finger along the side of my neck and then she said, "Are you okay if we get started?"

Get started? Hadn't they already started? If this wasn't starting, then what was it?

I gazed at Max again. He made eye contact with me and nodded, so I said, "Yes, how can I help?"

"Come this way," Betsey said. She led me to the master

bedroom, my *own* master bedroom, and she said, "Do you happen to have a loose-fitting robe? Something feminine that might suit him? We can take you shopping later, but this is such an impromptu occasion. We'll have to make do. Our plans this evening were to describe to you the way we like to dominate our men. The fact that Max gave us a visual to work with is really quite exciting."

That was one way to put things

I found a silky robe that was made of flowing, gossamer silk in a pattern of poppies and handed that over. Max had given me the robe for our first anniversary. I had satin slippers to go with it. These thoughts bubbled up in my head and popped one by one.

"Panties?" Betsey asked.

"None that would fit him."

She nodded, and then she smiled to herself as if she had come up with a winning idea.

"What?" I asked her, curious.

"No worries," she said, grabbing some of my makeup and the robe and then escorting me back down the hall.

I could hear the shower running and the sound of female voices. "Who's in there with him?" We paused outside the door. I could hear Tammy's voice and Lauren's, too. "What are they doing to him?"

"Probably shaving him. Maybe making him jerk off in front of them. I don't think they'll do an enema tonight. Not so soon."

"An enema," I repeated, dully. My heart felt as if someone had gripped around the organ with a fist--and I could feel its pulse beating between my legs, the heat swelling within my panties. I had to pause outside the door.

"They've got everything under control," Betsey promised me.

"Let's wait for them in the living room."

We returned to the space, and I looked around as if I'd never seen the room before. Look at those flowers. Who put them in the pretty vases? Couldn't have been me. Look at the sofa, so serene in that gold brocade. Had I perused bibles of patterns and fabric to choose that precise one? Anything that had happened before this night felt like a fantasy. Betsey seemed to understand my state of mind, because she kept me right next to her, and she held my hand and stroked my fingers, cooing soothing little noises to me from time to time.

While we waited, Donatella discussed how things had worked with her husband. "Tammy was the one who came up with the idea at first," she said. "I was unsure. It felt a little Stepford Wives to me, except flipped. You know? That women were in charge and then men were all in their frilly little pinafores and fancy panties."

God, why did her words turn me on so much? I tried to act as normal as I possibly could, but my pussy was so wet. I wondered if the other ladies could smell my scent.

"But see, she explained that a lot of men harbor this secret fantasy. They want to serve the women. They want to be put to use. With me and Bobby, well, we take turns. Sometimes I'm in charge and sometimes he is. With Tammy, there are no turns. She's always dominant. That's how she and her man like it."

The trio emerged then: Lauren, Max, and Tammy. Max was in a towel. He looked limp and damp. Tammy dried him off, a little roughly in my opinion, and when she patted his cock, he groaned.

"The boy's come twice for us," she explained to the rest of the party. "Don't let that groan fool you. He loved every second.

Especially, when Lauren fingerfucked that tight, slutty little asshole of his. She really reamed him good. It's going to fun to fit him for a plug, let me tell you. Or maybe..." she drifted off for a second. "Maybe we can have Bruce come over and drill him while we watch."

"And take pictures," Lauren said.

"Oh, god," Max murmured. It was one of the first things he'd said. All the women looked at him, and Lauren trilled a laugh and then said, "You want it bad, don't you, Maxie? You can't wait to feel big old Bruce's cock reaming your backdoor."

As she spoke, she pulled off his towel and started to stroke his cock again.

"We couldn't find any panties for Max," Betsey said.

"Not a problem," Tammy said, and she wriggled out of her own undergarments and handed them over to Max. That's not exactly what she did. She pressed them into his face and told him to breathe in deep. Then she had him put them on. "Bruce wears mine all the time," she said. So this is what Betsey had known would happen.

I had to shut my eyes and imagine that for a moment. I'd met Bruce several times. He was a built like a quarterback with dreamy blue eyes and a wicked smile. I wondered if perhaps that smile was because he had on a pair of ladies' undergarments beneath his chinos.

Tammy sat Max on the sofa and the women went to work on his makeup. They were obviously old hands at this, because in only a matter of minutes, they'd transformed him. With my eye pencil, blush, and shadows in place, he didn't look precisely female. But my husband definitely looked strikingly feminine.

"Now, I explained to Max what was going to happen," Tammy said. "But I'm not sure if he believed me."

She pushed Max back on the sofa and used her hand to rub him against the soft fabric of the panties.

"Once he's nice and hard again, we all get to take turns riding him. In every possible way. Like I said, when we're done, Bruce can come over and take care of the one place we're not physically equipped to handle."

"At least, not without a strap-on," said Lauren.

We all watched as Tammy stripped and climbed on top of my husband. I sat and stared, and then I felt Betsey's hand slip between my thighs to stroke my pussy. I pushed my hips forward, craving contact, as Tammy ground against Max's panty-covered cock.

"Oh, we are going to have fun with you," Tammy assured him. "We're going to take you slut-shopping in the city. We'll buy you filthy little hooker dresses. Lacy bras. Tight panties and fishnets. Stripper heels. A girly wig. An apron for serving us. Everything you could possibly need."

Max said, "Oh, god, yes. Please."

Tammy pulled down the waistband of the panties, revealing only the head of Max's cock. While I continued to stare, Donatella came closer and began to use the head like a lollipop, sucking on it so fiercely her cheeks indented.

Tammy rocked back a little, and I saw Donatella flick her tongue against Tammy's slit, and I grabbed Betsey's hand and thrust her fingers into my panties. I was giddy, so lightheaded from the situation I thought I'd come in no time at all. But part of me didn't want to. Not yet. Part of me wanted to wait and see what would happen next.

"Take them off," Tammy said, and Donatella pulled the panties of Max. Then, before anyone could stop her, Lauren got on first. She giggled at the look on Tammy and Donna's faces. "Don't worry, girls," she said. "They'll be plenty of timo for everyone."

She rode him fiercely, grinding her hips against his each time she settled down, then lifting up until she had only the tip of his cock in her pussy. Donatella watched this for several moments before forcefully demanding her own turn. I was surprised that Tammy allowed the women to take charge like this. I'd been struck by Tammy's power, and I thought for sure she'd eke out her own orgasm before sharing the wealth.

The doorbell rang then, and Lauren was the closest. She went to the door entirely naked and peeked through the peephole.

"Oh, it's Bruce," she called out to us as she opened the door. "Right on time," she added, and Max closed his eyes and moaned happily.

KINKING THE CLASSICS

THE PLANTER'S PUNCH

Nothing warms up an intimate gathering like a tall, cool breeze from the South Seas; a delicious punchbowl with a mix right from the islands mingles rums, senses and couples until the bowl runs dry. A bowl of Planter's Punch is the ideal icebreaker for all manner of entertaining, no matter how well you know your guests… at first sip, anyway.

Put on your sandals, turn Dean Martin up on the hi-fi, and get ready to play "how low can you go" with this kinky twist on Trader Vic's killer recipe from 1947. And dig that crazy color!

Ingredients

- 3 shots dark Jamaican rum
- 1 shot spiced rum
- 1 shot lime juice
- 1/2 shot lemon juice
- 1/2 shot grenadine
- 1/4-1/2 teaspoon superfine sugar

Instructions

Get your tall Collins glasses ready, and garnishes of any tropical delight you find at the market; a sliver of pineapple, slice of lime and a little fancy umbrella are always welcome on the rim of the glass. Put the whole kit and caboodle in a pitcher; stir well for 30 seconds with ice, then strain into a punchbowl. Serve over cracked ice.

REMOTE CONTROLLED

BY MELANIE DANIELS

I spent the first part of the evening telling Kirk no, I couldn't do it. I wouldn't do it. There was no possible way.

I spent the second part of the night doing it.

"You worry too much," Kirk chided me as he watched me gloss my lips.

"I like things to be perfect," I responded as I applied the raspberry shine.

"It will be perfect. I promise, baby. You'll have the perfect *O*. Better than you've ever had before."

See, Kirk had bought a brand-new, high-end remote-controlled vibrator. He surprised me with the toy right before our dinner party. I'd been in the midst of dressing, putting my hair up, fixing my makeup. The table was set. Vivaldi was on the stereo. Everything was ready. And that's when Kirk said, "Lie down on the bed and spread your legs, Lucy. I want to slip this egg up inside you."

His words made me instantly wet, but I told him no. There was no way. I was not going to let him hijack my dinner party. The one I'd planned for weeks. The one that was flawless in every conceivable way.

"You'll like this," he promised me.

"No, no, no!"

As I finished my preparations, he kept coming up and kissing me, teasing me, brushing his fingertips against my erect nipples through my melon-pink silk gown. "Come on, baby," he said. "What if I just lick your pussy a little, first?"

I'm sure he felt me pause. "Lick your pussy" in 'Kirk speak' meant that he would have me bucking and screaming on the bed in no time.

"Aha, my ice princess is melting." Kirk was in motion as soon as he sensed my shift in attitude, spreading me out on the mattress as if I were ripples of velvet. The fight had left my body. Kirk's crooning words combined with his bold embraces got the better of me, and finally I caved.

While my husband watched intently, I lifted my dress, bunching the sleek fabric in my fists until the hem was up to my waist. I stared down at him as he knelt and pulled my panties off and tossed them out of the way.

I held my breath, waiting for the moment when he'd start to do what he said. He winked at me, and then finally he bent and flicked my pussy with his tongue. He'd recently had his red hair cut short, and when I ran my palm over his scalp, he made a low growling noise in his throat, like a big cat. But soon I was the one really purring. Kirk is masterful with his mouth. He had me dripping in seconds as he made filthy spirals up and over my clit. I shut my eyes and fell back against the pillows in a mock swoon.

When Kirk goes down on me, I forget everything else. All I want is more—all I want is to feel the rotations of the tip of his tongue taking me higher. His magic tongue ultimately won me over to his side.

"Okay, you can put that thing in me. But you can't use the remote until after the guests leave."

Kirk worked my pussy more seriously now, preparing me for the new toy. He made me all drippy wet and then he slid the egg inside me. It was perfect, as he'd promised. A perfect fit.

That, I thought, was that.

I should have known better. Kirk loves his playthings. He owns a high-end, remote-controlled Model T and a helicopter that is perfectly to scale. Now he had a remote-controlled *me*. Why on earth had I thought he'd be able to wait? My man was like a big kid with a new toy. He couldn't keep his hands off his joystick.

The guests arrived right on time. Marla bounded in shaking droplets of rain off her ebony curls. "She refused to wear a raincoat," her husband complained. "She said she wanted to feel the weather on her." Suzanne was all wrapped up in a London Fog trench coat. Her shiny blonde hair was crystalline smooth. She had on high red rubber boots that she didn't take off. "It's part of my outfit," she insisted.

After leisurely sipping cocktails in our living room, the couples entered the dining room and sat at their assigned seats. I hadn't left anything to chance. I'd written name cards in calligraphy on crisp cream-colored folded cards. Salt and pepper shakers were stationed at every setting. I was the hostess with the mostess.

In more ways than one.

As I strode into the kitchen to prepare the appetizers, I felt a low rumble between my legs. It was as if someone had turned on an electric switch inside me—the motor took me by complete surprise. I hadn't exactly forgotten about the toy, but I'd lulled myself into thinking that Kirk would not use the device while our dining room was filled with our best friends.

No such luck. I arranged the appetizers on the little cola-colored glass plates and felt beads of sweat form at my temples. I wet a linen napkin and pressed the cool, heavy fabric to my face for a moment, willing myself to calm down. *Do not come*, I told myself. *Do not come in front of Bill and Marla and Suzanne and Doug. Do not come as you place the tiny little bitoo of smoked salmon in front of your guests.*

Thankfully, as I carried the plates back into the dining room, Kirk turned off the remote. I still had the egg tucked into my pussy, but the motor was off, and I could relax. Or at least, I could have a moment to regain my cool. I sat at the table with an audible sigh of relief, and I tucked into the dainty bites of gourmet food I'd worked so hard to prepare.

There was conversation around the table. We'd all known each other since college, so the chatter came easily. I was fooled once more into thinking that Kirk would behave. Why did I think that? Honestly, I don't know. He's never behaved before.

When I cleared the plates to prepare for the first course, the buzzer went off again. This time, Kirk hit me right as I was entering the kitchen, and I hoped that the sounds of the banter drowned out the low rumble of the motor tucked into my snatch. I could easily imagine one of our guests asking what the noise was. And what could I possibly say? "Kirk's got a new toy," was all I could think of.

"Do you need any help?" Suzanne called out to me.

"No, no, I'm fine," I assured her as the door shut behind me. The power of the vibrator had increased. Kirk was playing fast and loose with his new gizmo, learning the various levels. I thought of the time he'd stayed up all night breaking in a new video game. He'd told me he couldn't sleep until he'd mastered every step.

I leaned against the chrome refrigerator and breathed deep and slow, like I do in yoga class. I could not believe how intense this felt. I'd used a vibrator occasionally, but I'd almost always focused on rubbing the tip of the toy against my clit. Having the egg thrust up inside me, whirring away from within, was by far the most erotic thing that I'd ever experienced.

Behind my shut lids, I saw starbursts of violet and cinnamon and saffron. The pleasure was growing stronger with each passing second. I put my palm against the front of my pussy and pressed forward. I only needed a little more stimulation and I would reach the…

"Lucy!" Kirk called innocently from the dining room. "Everything okay in there?"

Oh, he sounded like the concerned husband, didn't he? When he knew full well that I was doing my best to stave off a world-class orgasm. I tend to be loud when I climax. What would our guests think if they heard me moaning in the kitchen? Could I make them believe I was disheartened by a fallen soufflé?

With trembling hands, I arranged the first course and brought the plates out to the diners. Kirk continued to play his nasty tricks on me. Our swinging door between the kitchen and dining room seemed to be the gateway of truth. When I entered the kitchen, I'd feel that egg buzzing to life. When I returned to the dining room, the power would slowly recede to nothing, and I'd be left limp and useless in my chair.

After several of these occurrences, I realized my attitude had shifted. I was actually looking forward to the movements of the vibrator inside me. When Marla dropped her fork, I practically sprinted to the kitchen to grab her a new utensil. And I didn't hurry to rush back to the table. I called out, "I'll just wash this for you," and I let the hot water go to steaming before I soaped, rinsed, and dried the antique implement. The whole time, I felt myself growing closer to climax as Kirk played me like one of his favorite video games, shooting the asteroids of my pleasure.

Marla gave me a slightly odd look when I returned, her cupid's bow lips pursed in confusion, and I realized I didn't have her fork in hand. Whoops. I'd left the kitchen in such a state of sublime delight I'd forgotten why I'd even been there.

"One sec," I told her, returning to grab the fork. Sadly, there was no instant buzzing in my pussy. Had Kirk grown tired of the game? Apparently so, because he entered the kitchen a moment later and said, "You start getting the main course ready. I'll bring Marla her fork." As he spoke, the vibrator clicked onto high without warning. My whole body shivered, and I stared at him in awe. He wasn't holding the device. He had no way to be pressing the button. What was going on?

"I gave the remote to Doug. I didn't think you'd mind."

That denoted the end of the dining portion of our party—and the beginning of the real entertainment.

"You gave the control to Doug?" I asked, making sure I'd heard him correctly.

"But he probably handed it to Suzanne," Kirk said, smiling.

I couldn't talk any more. The toy was bringing me white-hot waves of pleasure. I clutched onto Kirk and held him while I came.

The orgasm was like none that I'd ever experienced before, probably in part because of the thought of Suzanne working the device. I shook all over at the power of the vibrations, and Kirk embraced me the entire time, kissing my cheeks, licking my lips. He extended the sweet gratification that flowed through my body, his big hands roaming all over me, his full lips decorating me with kisses. When the climax was over, that motor still rumbled.

"It's too much," I whispered to him. "I can't take it."

Kirk didn't seem to care about the next course. He lifted me in his arms and carried me back to the dining room. As he sat me down in my chair, I realized something unusual was going on. The other women at the party had taken their stockings and panties off. Marla was bent over the table while Doug inserted an egg into her pussy. Suzanne was on her back on the floor, scarlet boots still on, and Bill had her legs over his shoulders. He was rubbing another egg directly onto her clit, and she was writhing under his touch and sighing deeply at the sensation.

"I bought extras," Kirk explained to me, stating the obvious. "Like party favors. I hope you don't mind."

How could I mind? The sexual escapades had started so naturally, and the women looked seriously aroused as the men began to toy with the remotes. I saw that Suzanne did, indeed, have my remote in her hand. She and I made eye contact as she dialed down the power on my device. I sat there for a moment, staring in awe as the partiers entertained themselves.

Kirk went to Marla who got on her hands and knees on the floor. She opened her mouth automatically as he opened his fly, and she started to suck his cock with gusto. Her short black curls bobbed as she moved and her diamond hoops sparkled in the light, but it was Kirk's thick manhood that captivated my attention. I had a sudden epiphany that he must have been hard all evening from playing with me. While I'd experienced release—he was still dangerously erect. Marla moaned around my man's mammoth dick, and the sound of her voice dropped into a deeper timber as Doug started to rim her.

I turned my attention to Suzanne and Bill. Blonde and bubbly Suzi winked at me, and suddenly I felt flutters of desire beginning to grow within me once more. Suzi was playing with my button, and I stood and moved closer to her so that I could watch as Bill fucked her. When Bill handed me her remote, we were truly entwined. I was in charge of her contentment. She had her fist around my bliss.

Game on.

Rather than put the device up inside Suzanne, Bill had simply let the egg rest on top of her clit. I pressed firmly on the orb, holding it in place as I made the happy toy begin to gyrate.

Without a word, we began to engage in a war to see which one of us would make the other come first. At least, that's what I thought the battle was. Perhaps she thought we were each trying to beat the other to climax. It didn't really matter. Both of us would undoubtedly win in the end. Suzanne cranked up the power of the vibrations inside me. I did the same to hers. Bill continued to pound her pussy. I turned my head and saw that Kirk was now fucking Marla while she sucked her own juices off Doug.

Bill caught my attention by flipping Suzi onto her stomach and entering her from behind. The egg fell to the floor. I grabbed it up and placed the humming toy against her asshole. She seemed to appreciate that, because she started to cry out—her voice louder than any other sound in the room.

"Let her lick your pussy," Bill instructed.

He didn't have to tell me twice. I got into position in front of her, and Suzi began to nip and tug at my clit. When Bill thrust into her extra hard, her mouth pushed forcefully against my throbbing core, and I came almost unexpectedly. The waves never ceased inside me. They ebbed and flowed, crashing again and again, until I felt completely demolished.

I moved aside to let the couple grind out their own pleasure. The egg was still up in me, and Suzi seemed to have forgotten she was supposed to be handling my remote. Kirk, after coming all over Marla's face and chest, went to snag the device. Mussed beyond reason, I leaned back against the wall, holding myself upright through sheer will as the largest orgasm I'd had all evening finally broke.

"Oh, god," I whispered, under my breath. Kirk got on his knees in front of me, and he started to tickle my split with his tongue as I came from the vibrations. "That's so good," I said, stating the obvious, but unable to keep quiet.

Kirk licked me until I had to push him away. Then he said, "Go get the lube, baby doll. Marla wants me to fuck her ass while the egg is in her pussy."

I walked slowly down the hall listening to the cadence of sighs and moans emanating from the dining room.

Yet another dinner party in our intimate little couple's social club had taken an unexpected turn.

But somehow I was sure our guests didn't mind.

GOOD HOUSEKEEPING

TIPS FOR CLEANING YOUR TOYS

Your kitchen has everything you need to keep your playthings clean and ready for action. What your toys are made up determines how, and if, they can be properly cleaned for going another round in the ring.

Most commercially available sex toys are made from plastic, jelly rubber, silicone, glass, vinyl, "softskin" or plastic.

Porous toys are jelly rubber and "softskin" (as well as fake silicone, aka 'siligel') and they're difficult to clean completely; consider them disposable after they get dull on the surface. Clean them with unscented antibacterial soap (like Hibiclens) or a solution of 1:10 bleach and water, though alcohol and water works just fine. Clean plastics, wood and other items similarly.

Non-porous materials, such as silicone, metal, porcelain, and glass sex toys are wonderfully easy to clean. A wipe-down or a swish in 1:10 bleach (or alcohol) to water, antibacterial soap, or dish soap suds for two minutes get these play pals squeaky clean and ready for more. Silicone can go the extra distance for complete cleanliness; boil your silicone for 3-5 minutes or run it in the top rack of the dishwasher for complete sterilization.

Just don't forget to unload your "special housewares" from the dish rack before anyone else helps out in the kitchen. Unless it's all part of your domestic plan, of course.

EGGSHELL, ECRU AND LINEN

BY DANTE DAVIDSON

The retro telephone sound on my computer alerted me to the fact that I had an incoming Skype call. I checked the number. Sheila. It was a busy day around the office, and I didn't have time to see her new paint chips. She'd been tormenting me for weeks with this hue or that, all apparently the same color. In my eyes, eggshell is ecru is linen. But to Sheila, each shade was decidedly different, and the difference could make or break our bedroom.

Seven times a day. Barely Beige. Dove Wing. Light Breeze. Shakespeare Tan.

Seriously? *Shakespeare Tan.* Someone got paid to create that name. Think about that for a moment.

The truth was that I didn't care. Sheila *knew* I didn't care. I'd gone beyond *pretending* to care.

I answered the call with an impatient sigh, I'll admit that. The (paint) chips were down, so to speak. I was fifty shades past the ability to comment. And I stayed that way. Because what I saw when the Skype window opened was Sheila tied to our antique four-poster bed. There were three men in the room, men I'd never seen before.

One was dark-haired and tall, with vibrantly colored tattoos spiraling all over his pale skin. Another had blond hair to his shoulders and was what I'd consider a surfer type, a real all-American stud. The last was slightly off-screen.

I could only see his big dick aimed right at my wife's face.

"Hi, Honey," Sheila said, and she flittered her fingers at me. She couldn't actually wave. Not tied down like that.

I think I said *Hello*. I might have grunted. The men were naked. Each one of them was massive. I'd never seen men like that before outside of porn flicks. I'm not out of shape by any means, but I'm not a human mountain, either.

"The painters are here," Sheila cooed, stating the obvious. There were ladders in the room and splattered drop cloths on the floor. And then there was Sheila. I could see her shaved snatch. I could see how wet she was. The juices were glossy all over her beautiful bare pussy lips.

"Yeah," I said, agreeing with her statement. *The painters were definitely there.*

"This one's Roger. Say hi to my husband, Roger." Roger was the dark-haired one. He cocked his head in my direction and then he bent and started to kiss my wife. I felt my breath catch. We'd shared fantasies like this in the past. I'd been open with Sheila, telling her that there was nothing that would turn me on more than seeing her in the heart of a gangbang. But that she'd gone and done this was more romantic than anything I could imagine.

When Roger pulled back, Sheila appeared slightly dazed. She shook her pretty head and then said, "That's Troy."

Troy was the surfer. He didn't even glance at me. Instead, he climbed onto the mattress and straddled Sheila's body. I could guess that she was blowing him based on the slurpy sounds she was making, but all I could see was his rear view, his asscheeks tightening and releasing as pleasure flowed through him. Bound like that, Sheila had no choice but to keep sucking him until he moved aside. The third man entered the frame now, looking directly at the camera. He had the kind of knowing smirk on his face that made me feel as if he could read my thoughts. He didn't let Sheila introduce him. He said, "I'm Matthew. Nice to meet you, Mr. Williams."

I stared at him, taking in his crew cut, deep green eyes, ripped body. I felt overdressed in my suit. The four of them were so strikingly naked. But I found it in myself to say, "Hey Matthew." I couldn't add the *Nice to meet you*. Not when he was about to fuck my wife.

After the introductions were over, the men didn't seem to care much about the camera pointed in their direction. Roger moved to the foot of the foot of the bed, and he started tickling Sheila's feet. She sucked in air and her body went tense. My pretty wife has a thing for being bound and tortured. I didn't know precisely what she'd told the men, but they seemed to understand her fetish instinctively. Sheila giggled, and the man tickled faster. The two other painters came closer to Sheila. She gripped onto Matthew's cock and leaned forward—as far as she could within the restraints.

She clearly wanted to suck him, the slut. But in her position, she couldn't connect. Matthew laughed at her and ran his thumb along her bottom lip. She drew his digit into her mouth and began to suck on that instead.

Big blond Troy worked his dick into Sheila's hand, and she tightened her fist and began to jack him off while Matthew moved forward. He teased her, smacking her lips with the head of his cock.

She stuck her tongue into the slit of the cock in her face.

Oh, if I could only have been there in person. I would have orchestrated the entire scene. I would have told each man what to do. Where to stand. How to touch my wife to bring her the greatest amount of pleasure. As it was, I was a helpless voyeur, captured in my desk chair, focused on the X-rated movie unfolding in real time on my screen.

I had the wherewithal to stand and lock my office door. Then I sat back down and watched. In my absence of only a second, the scene had already changed. Roger was now between Sheila's legs. Was he licking her pussy? Was he tonguing her box? I heard Sheila squeal, and then I heard a familiar tapping sound. She'd given him one of our toys, a slapper made specifically for pussy spanking. He was warming her up, and I wanted to scream at the players to move so I could see better. *Down in front! Go to the left! I need to see!*

I held my tongue barely, and watched as the trio of men began to work over my wife. They seemed to require greater access, too, because in only a few minutes, they unbound her and positioned her on her hands and knees. She was ass toward the camera now, so I couldn't see her face. I was a little sad about that, but not too sad.

With Sheila in this position, I was able to watch her ass redden as Troy delivered a bum-blistering spanking with Sheila's favorite paddle. Sheila would have cried out. I know the sounds she makes when I punish her sweet peach-split of an ass. But she couldn't. Not blowing the dark-haired painter like that. Roger had gotten in front of her and was gripping onto her short birch-blonde hair and helping her find the rhythm he desired. I heard her gag a little around the girth of his cock, and I unzipped my own slacks and got a hand around my Johnson.

"Look how she arches her back for the next spank," the tattooed stud observed. "She's such a little pain slut."

"Why don't you put it in her ass, then?" asked Matthew.

"After I spank her a little more. See, she gave me this…" the blond was holding something I recognized intimately: a paint chip. I bit down on a laugh. Sheila had given her punisher a stiff card that featured five different shades of red. I could see that one of the hues was circled. The painter spanked Sheila a few more times and then held the paint chip against her ass.

"Perfect," he said, and Sheila moaned in agreement.

"Lube, dude?" the dark-haired man offered the blond.

"Wait… wait," said Matthew. To my delight, he was a wise ass. He grabbed a new brush, the type used for fine detailing, and he lubed up the bristles. While the surfer held open Sheila's asscheeks, Matthew started to paint lube all around her anus. *Oh, God.* My precome was leaking out of my dick now. Who would have thought to use a brush like that? Sheila was mewling around the dark-haired painter's cock. She was moaning and sighing but never letting go of the dick in her mouth. At least, not until the next painter wanted his turn. The men tussled for a second, vying for position…

"I'm taking her ass," said the blond. "I need to be in this hole." He started to finger her asshole as he spoke, and I just bet that Sheila was on the cusp of her first climax. She can come from having her anus stimulated. And now with her choice of cocks in front of her, she must have felt transported.

"Back and forth," the blond told her. "You suck Roger and then

Matthew. See which one you can get off first." He wanted her to take the cocks in turn, but Sheila seemed to have another idea. She motioned for the men to move together as she tried to get two cockheads in her mouth at once. *My greedy girl.*

The blond got ready to fuck her ass now, lubing up his dick until his skin shone with the glistening liquid. I was working my hand on my cock so fast now. But I was worried. If he took her ass like this, I would only see his rear view again. I wouldn't be able to see Sheila at all.

She seemed to understand that, even if the men didn't. Or maybe they did, but they didn't care. She moved so she was sideways, and now I got to see her bobbing back and forth between the two studs, sucking one cock then the other, back and forth. She was waggling her ass at the surfer boy until he gripped her hips, held her steady, and pinned her with his cock in her hole.

"Ohhhhhh…." Sheila had to stop blowing the men in order to let loose with a wicked groan. The trio laughed. There was no mistaking the pleasure in that sound.

For a few strokes, the blond simply worked his manhood into her tight back door. Then he did something that surprised me and Sheila at the same time. He lifted her up, supporting her body against his. Then he motioned to one of the other painters. He didn't seem to care which one. The brunette inched forward, and he helped turn Sheila into the sexiest sandwich I'd ever seen. He impaled her in the front while the blond took her back door.

That left the third at loose ends. Poor boy.

But not, it turned out, for long.

Matthew circled the bed, as if looking for a way in. Then he said,

"Heads or tails, Roger. Heads or tails?"

What was he talking about?

The brunette said, "Tails," and I expected somehow for one of them to produce a coin and flip for some unnamed prize, but the man simply picked up the lube and started to slick up Roger's backdoor.

Oh, god. They were going to fuck my wife in tandem. Matthew got in position behind Roger who was in her pussy, against the blond who was in her ass. I came then. I came so hard, I cried out. The four people all looked over toward the camera, and I felt naked and exposed. Fuck. They could see me. I'd managed to forget that. But honestly, I didn't care. I kept jerking my messy cock as Matthew proceeded to fuck Roger who never stopped railing against my wife. Troy kept at it from his end, until the foursome started to come in the sweetest chain-reaction I'd ever seen.

Troy came first, filling Sheila's back hole with his seed. Matt was next, doing the same to Roger's ass. Roger and Sheila seemed to come together, pressed against one another, grinding out their bliss.

All was quiet for a few moments, except for the panting of their breathing. Then the men pulled out of my wife—and each other—and stood nearby the bed. Sheila told them where the bathroom was, so that they could go and clean up. Then she faced the camera, a look of sublime satisfaction on her face.

"Did you get painters who could fuck?" I asked when the men left the room.

"No, baby. Porn stars who could paint. Much easier. I didn't care so much about their prowess with a paintbrush as with their cocks."

"Well, I think you got your money's worth," I said, looking her over. She positively glowed.

"Do you like the walls, honey?" she asked, her mascara was streaking down her face. "I had them do each one different, so you could choose."

I glanced at the walls and saw that I still couldn't tell the colors apart. Shaker Deer Path. Putty.

"Whatever you think is best," I said, my voice choked with emotion. "I'll leave the decision to you."

ABOUT THE AUTHORS

Melanie Daniels finds dinner parties boring. She had the idea for "Remote Controlled" while sitting next to the dullest man in the world at a recent six-course meal.

Dante Davidson's short stories have appeared in anthologies including *Bondage*, *Naughty Stories from A to Z*, *Best Bondage Erotica*, *The Merry XXXmas Book of Erotica*, *Luscious* and *Sweet Life*. With Alison Tyler, he is the coauthor of *Bondage on a Budget* and *Secrets for Great Sex After 50*.

Amelia Monroe is a professor's wife. She is also a professor. Although jazz has never been her scene, she enjoys making love to the sounds of classical, soul, and old-school rock.

Emilie Paris's first novel, *Valentine* was made into an audiotape by Passion Press. She abridged the seventeenth-century novel, *The Carnal Prayer Mat* for Passion Press, which won a Publisher's Weekly best audio award in the "Sexcapades" category.

Jewel Rodriguez recently moved to the suburbs from a large, metropolitan city. She is still trying to get used to lawns, block parties, and neighbors who greet her on the street.

Alison Tyler (@alisontyler, alisontyler.blogspot.com) is naughty and she knows it. Her sultry short stories have appeared in more than 100 anthologies including *Coupling* edited by Sommer Marsden and *Sex for America* edited by Stephen Elliott. She is the author of more than 25 erotic novels, including the upcoming *The Pet*, and the editor of more than 75 explicit anthologies, including *Smart Ass* and *Kiss My Ass*. Visit alisontyler.com 24/7 as she's a total insomniac. Support her writing on Patreon.

Tasha Waters is a bisexual actress-cum-writer who has hidden her addiction to needlepoint until now. She can cross-stitch with the best of them but she's only learning the closed featherstitch. All her profits go to thread.

ABOUT THE EDITOR

Ms. Violet Blue (@violetblue, tinynibbles.com) is a cybersecurity columnist at Engadget and has reported on cybercrime for many outlets including CNET, Zero Day, ZDNet, and CBS News. She has authored and edited over 40 award-winning, best-selling books in eight translations. The London Times named Violet Blue one of "40 bloggers who really count."

Blue has reported on hacking, cybercrime and privacy violations and tech's impact on at-risk populations in countries including Malaysia, Thailand, Germany, Russia, China, the Dominican Republic, the United States and UK, Norway and Serbia. Her work as a journalist has broken many large stories about hacking and cybercrime, affecting the largest online companies and millions of users. Blue is the journalist who broke the story when Anonymous hacked The US Federal Reserve Bank, the Google "nymwars" story, the event in which social sharing app Snapchat was hacked and user database exposed, and when Comcast was hacked and millions of user accounts were compromised. She is also responsible for breaking many critical stories in which Apple iMessage and Apple iCloud were shown to be hackable, and when hackers showed how to hack an Apple iPhone in 60 seconds.

She has been at the center of many Internet scandals, including Google's "nymwars" and Libya's web domain censorship and seizures—Forbes calls her "omnipresent on the web" and named her a Forbes Web Celeb. She has given talks at such conferences as ETech, The Oslo Freedom Forum, and the Forbes Brand Leadership Conference, she received a standing ovation at Seattle's Gnomedex, and has given two Tech Talks at Google. In 2012, Blue presented "Hackers and Harm Reduction" on the featured stage for CCC's 29c3 [Europe's largest] hacker conference in Hamburg, Germany.

If you enjoyed Filthy Housewives, please consider doing us a favor: Can you take a minute to leave a review wherever you happened to pick it up? Also, please tell a friend about our books. Online retailers are making it harder than ever to find quality erotica, and anything you can do to help spread the word about our books and these fine authors would be amazing. We're lucky we get to write and create these ridiculous, sex-positive, celebratory books, but unless we can reach readers, it's almost pointless.

Thank you for reading our smutty little book! If you'd like to read more erotica collections with the same quality and sensibilities as this one, check out more from Digita Publications. You may also enjoy Bent Over His Desk: Hot Office Kink, Filthy Housewives, Bisexual Husbands, and Wetware: Cyberpunk Erotica.

Digita Publications is my indie store where you'll find self-published works and buy them direct: All authors are paid directly. Digita Publications strives for a world in which book publishing embraces transparency, and audiobooks are DRM free and unrestricted by corporate monopolies. All Digita ebooks and audiobooks are intended for sharing and unrestricted use. Follow @digitapub on Twitter for updates.

Bisexual Husbands: Seven Stories of Men Who Can't Resist

These *Bisexual Husbands* have cravings for a same-sex tryst, and their wives can't wait to watch—or join in, sometimes controlling the action. Layered characters and vivid, clever fantasies drive this compendium of bisexual men in loving couples who want to get dirty—sometimes taking turns as the center of a three-way where there's truly no limits.

This rich anthology is artfully spiked with charming cocktail recipes and playful tips for trying out bisexual fantasies in real life. Blue's introduction "Bisexual and Voracious" takes apart what everyone gets wrong about bi men—namely, that they don't really exist. This book shows exactly how hot bisexual men can be.

Bent Over His Desk: Hot Office Kink

If you wished the film *Secretary* went all the way, *Bent Over His Desk: Hot Office Kink* gives you what you need.

Enter a workplace where rules are broken, collars are mussed, and erotic punishment is swift—and satisfying. Bestselling editor and author Alison Tyler applies her erudite erotic curation skills to the topic of sex at the office, resulting in a volume of stories equal parts sexually explicit and utterly compelling.

These eleven splendidly kinky tales of sex at the office twist, turn, arouse and inspire in ways that only today's best erotica authors can deliver: Tyler brings together experts of the craft including

Sommer Marsden, Alison Tyler, Thomas S. Roche, Sophia Valenti, Dante Davidson, and more.

Wetware: Cyberpunk Erotica

Cyberpunk anti-heroes face global conspiracies, misused government R&D, thugs, drugs, true love, artificial intelligence, and vengeful sexbots in *Wetware*.

Love is a side effect of stolen, weaponized biotech in *Bishop to King's Pawn, Two* by Thomas S. Roche. A brainwave hacker's conquest in a bathroom stall takes a turn in Cecilia Tan's *Rough, Trade*. Lines are crossed when the household bot in Devyn X. Sands' *Never Say No* has enough of her owner's perversions. *Sixty-Five Night* by Stephen Stavros charts an AI experiment that pushes one woman into edgy transhuman sex, under the shadow of a murder conspiracy.

Wetware is a tech-savvy, philosophically rich, erotic anthology artfully spiked with cyberpunk-themed cocktails and hotlists of sexy cyberpunk films, books, and anime.

Printed in Great Britain
by Amazon